PUFFIN B

TARONGA

Two years after Last Days, Australia has become a dangerous place, and a battleground for survival.

Ben, who has a telepathic ability to control animals, leads a hazardous existence in the bush west of the Blue Mountains. Hopeful of a kinder life in the city, he escapes to Sydney – only to be further disillusioned. Then, at the heart of the city, he comes upon Taronga Zoo, which has been strangely unaffected by the general chaos. Or has it? Is it an island of safety in the midst of so much danger? Or is it really the most sinister place of all?

Named an Honour Book in the 1987 Children's Book of the Year Awards, *Taronga* is another gripping novel from one of Australia's most outstanding writers.

ALSO BY VICTOR KELLEHER

TARONGA

VICTOR KELLEHER

PUFFIN BOOKS

Puffin Books
Penguin Books Australia Ltd
487 Maroondah Highway, PO Box 257
Ringwood, Victoria 3134, Australia
Penguin Books Ltd Harmondsworth, Middlesex, England
Viking Penguin, A Division of Penguin Books USA Inc.
375 Hudson Street, New York, New York 10014, USA
Penguin Books Canada Limited
10 Alcorn Avenue, Toronto, Ontario, Canada M4V 3B2
Penguin Books (N.Z.) Ltd
182-190 Wairau Road, Auckland 10, New Zealand

First published by Viking Kestrel Australia, 1986
Published by Puffin Books, 1988
This edition published 1990
13 15 17 19 20 18 16 14
Copyright © Victor Kelleher, 1986

Offset from the Viking Kestrel edition
Made and printed in Australia by McPherson's Printing Group, Maryborough, Victoria

National Library of Australia
Cataloguing-in-Publication data:

Kelleher, Victor, 1939–
Taronga.
ISBN 0 14 032631 6.
I. Title.
A823.3

The quotation from *To the Islands* by Randolph Stow is
reproduced with the kind permission of Angus & Robertson

'You love the things you kill,' Heriot said, 'but you never regret killing them. I've noticed that always about you people, how you love your prey. There's some wisdom there.'

Randolph Stow, *To the Islands*

PART I

THE CALLING

CHAPTER ONE

Ben crept stealthily down the hillside, picking his way between the boulders and young gums, making for the cover of a straggly line of river oaks. From there he had a clear view of the creek below. It appeared almost deserted, only a small flock of brightly coloured finches drinking from the brackish thread of water that snaked along the sandy bed. And yet he was certain that he had received a response to his earlier Call – that something big was hiding down there, waiting for him.

He Called again. Not aloud; making the sound in his mind. And straight away he spotted her: a big female roo, an Eastern Grey, less than ten metres from where he stood; her bulky body so evenly streaked with sunlight and shadow that she had been invisible until then. Only the sudden movement of her head, as she responded to the Call, had given her away. She was watching him now, her large eyes showing no fear or distrust, her body relaxed and still.

It was a situation he was all too familiar with and he glanced quickly over his shoulder, up towards the ridge. The swell of the hillside hid Greg from view, but Ben knew he was there, rifle at the ready, his thin wolfish face intent on the open creek bed. Without needing to think about what must happen next, Ben stepped over the cable-like roots of a tall river oak and walked towards the unshaded strip of sand. He

3

had learned from long experience that the roo, lulled by his Call, would ignore her instinctive fear of the open sunlight and follow him.

Sure enough, as he passed her she leaned forward into the characteristic shuffling gait of her kind. That was when he noticed her pouch, saw it out of the corner of his eye: the furred skin heavily distended; the head and one hind leg of a half-grown joey poking up out of the opening.

He stopped then and faced her. The tall upright figure of the roo and the slightly built figure of the fourteen-year-old boy only a pace or two apart. He, momentarily undecided; she, watching him with trusting eyes.

'Go on,' he said quietly, acting on an impulse too strong to resist, 'get out of here.'

She shied at the sound of his voice.

'Shoo!' he said more loudly. 'Clear off!'

When she still hesitated he sent out a silent warning, signifying danger.

That was too much for her. With a sinuous movement, she turned and bounded away through the scrub that lined the creek, leaving the boy alone in the depths of the valley.

Despite the warmth of the spring afternoon, Ben shivered and drew the ragged remains of his shirt closed across his chest. As if to bolster his flagging courage, he hitched his equally ragged shorts up around his waist before reluctantly raising his eyes towards the ridge where Greg would still be watching – and saw with relief that the line of river oaks had prevented either himself or the roo from being spotted. That was something to be thankful for. He could always claim later that he had been mistaken, that the valley had been empty all along. Greg wouldn't be pleased, but he'd be unlikely to burst into a rage.

Ben turned away, meaning to climb back up the hillside – and at that moment detected another response to his earlier Call. It was further off and it came this time not from a roo,

4

but from something else. He stopped and scanned the opposite slope. He had to wait several minutes before he caught a flash of movement near the top of the ridge; a mere glimpse of fawn and brown, gone before he could identify it. He knew only that it was a reasonably small animal, low enough to the ground to be hidden by the tall grass and young gums that covered the hillside; its rapid, winding descent marked by the waving of the unripe seed-heads.

Suddenly uneasy, Ben issued a probing Call. Instantly the movement on the hillside stopped and the pointed snout and prick-ears of a young dingo appeared above the grass. Without hesitation, Ben sent out the same warning signal he had used earlier on the roo. But in this case it had a very different effect. The dingo, like himself and Greg, was a hunter, and instead of running away, it leaped onto a shelf of rock in order to survey the valley more clearly.

'No!' Ben yelled, and began running, his bare feet floundering in the soft yellow sand of the creek bed.

He could see the dingo immediately above him, its coat a deep gold in the sunlight, its head cocked curiously to one side. Its eyes, he noticed, conveyed a sense not of alarm, but of trust. That self-same trust which, over the past months, had come to haunt him.

'Get away . . . !' he began.

And then the rifle shot filled the valley. A violent gush of sound that forced the dingo to its knees and rolled it off the rock, down into the long grass.

When Ben reached the animal it was still alive, though panting heavily, its tongue lolling from its mouth. The wound must have been on its other side because the golden fur was unblemished. It might almost have been lying there resting. Only its eyes revealed its true condition: they were oddly filmed over, already fixed upon that invisible darkness which was steadily engulfing it.

Ben crouched beside the dying animal, aware that he could

do nothing to save it now – that in a sense he had done too much already. After a few minutes he heard hurried footsteps behind him and he stood up and turned. Greg was clambering up towards him, the rifle gripped in one hand.

'Did I get it?' he asked excitedly.

Like Ben, he was a ragged figure, dressed in the worn-out remains of old clothes. But there the similarity between them ended, because he was much bigger and older than Ben, probably in his late teens or early twenties: a tall, heavy-boned young man with a fierce, uncompromising face.

'Yeah, you got it,' Ben answered quietly, 'but it's not dead yet.'

Greg grinned at him, the skin around his mouth scarred by sores, his teeth broken and discoloured. 'We'll soon fix that,' he said, reversing the gun so that he now held it like a club.

'Couldn't you just shoot it?' Ben asked. 'You know . . . quick.'

The grin vanished from Greg's face. 'Where d'you think I get ammo from? Trees?'

Behind him, Ben could hear the dingo's quick, frantic gasps. 'Only one shot,' he pleaded.

Greg grasped an old tree-stump to steady himself on the steep hillside. 'Listen, kid,' he said threateningly, 'you've done your job, what I feed you for. Now leave me to do mine.'

Again he advanced up the slope, head lowered purposefully; and Ben, before he could think about what he was doing, stepped directly into his path. It was the first time, in the two long years he had spent with Greg, that he had openly defied him.

'What!' Greg burst out angrily, that one word more like a snarl than a human sound. 'D'you wanna join the oldies? Is that it?'

'Please, Greg,' he whined, 'be a mate. Just this once.' He cringed as he spoke, putting on an act that had often saved him in the past.

6

'Get out!' Greg shouted, his face going livid, flecks of foam appearing at the corners of his mouth. And when Ben failed to move quickly enough, he swung the butt of the rifle viciously.

Ben never actually felt the impact. There was a brief pause, with the sound of the dingo's panting breaths swelling out over the hillside, as if the sky itself were struggling to breathe. Then the shadows and the sunlight clashed together, bending the earth beneath his feet. For an instant everything appeared incredibly bright and clear. The shadows were still there, at the edge of his vision, waiting to engulf him as they would the dingo. But not yet. And in that last instant of consciousness, as the heavy butt of the rifle jerked his head sideways, he at last grasped what was happening.

'I'm like the dingo,' he thought in astonishment, 'the two of us ... the same ...'

It may have been the discomfort which roused him. He came to and realized dimly that he was being carried, drooped uncomfortably across Greg's shoulder. At each step his aching head was jolted painfully and he clenched his eyes tight-closed, willing himself back into the peaceful darkness which welled up around him like calm soothing water.

After that he must have slept naturally, because when he next awoke he felt better. Night had fallen and he was lying in their makeshift hut, the firelight flickering on the bark walls. For a while he lay still, feeling tense and confused, unable to recall what had happened. Then he saw the slack, bloodied dingo skin hanging on the far wall, and the events of the afternoon came rushing back. The skin, he observed bitterly, was no longer smooth and golden: without the living body to give it vitality and form, it was little more than a loose brown rag.

Holding one hand to the swollen side of his head, he sat up. Greg was crouched beside the fire, cooking the remains of their previous kill, the slightly 'high' meat filling the hut with a sickly smell.

'What did you go and shoot it for?' he asked quietly.

Greg swung round, his face obscured by shadow. 'You all right?'

'Not bad. Why'd you kill it?'

Greg turned back to his cooking. 'It's a good bit of leather,' he said, speaking over his shoulder. 'It'll come in handy when we have to chuck out these clothes.'

Ben crawled over to the fire, so he could see Greg's face. 'You've said that before,' he reminded him, 'but we always ditch the skins when we move on.'

The older boy shrugged indifferently, his hard, lean face revealing nothing. 'So what?' he answered.

'So there was no need to kill it.'

Greg poked at the meat with the bent prongs of an old fork. 'Dingoes eat the same food as us,' he said shortly. 'I reckon that's reason enough.'

'Not for me.'

'Then that's your bad luck.'

'No, it's yours,' Ben responded quickly, 'because I'm leaving.'

He expected Greg to flare out at him. Instead he took a burning stick from the fire and held it between them in an oddly threatening gesture.

'You know what happened last time,' he said softly, the suggestion of a smile on his face.

Ben could hardly have forgotten. Within four hours of running off, Greg had caught up with him and beaten him so badly it had taken him a month to recover.

'I'm still going,' he said doggedly.

'Suit yourself.'

'I will.'

Again he was ready for a show of anger, but the older boy merely speared a piece of cooked meat and handed it to him.

It tasted old and gamy, but that was a taste he'd grown used to and he ate it gladly enough. As soon as he'd finished he took one of the plastic mugs and crawled out through the low doorway.

Outside it was moonless and dark, with a cool wind blowing from the south, rustling the gum leaves overhead. He paused long enough to check the sky, noting with satisfaction that although it was mainly clear, there was a heavy mass of cloud on the southern horizon. Unexpectedly, that line of cloud reminded him of a similar scene years earlier. The sky wider, because he'd been out at sea, somewhere off Sydney Heads: his mother standing by the tiller of the boat; he and his father crouched in the bows, whistling up the wind. With a sense of surprise, he realized that must have been his first conscious act of Calling. Yet still it wasn't wise to dwell on such memories, and he quickly repressed it and made his way down to the creek.

Here, too, the water was low, a narrow thread winding across the sand. Only one sizable pool remained, and he drank from this and afterwards ducked his aching head into its soothing coolness. As he rocked back onto his heels, dribbles of water coursing down his face and neck, he heard a faint noise behind him.

'It's all right,' he called, 'I'm not trying to sneak off.'

Greg emerged from the darkness and squatted beside him. 'How d'you think you'd cope out there on your own?' he asked, vaguely indicating the surrounding bush.

'I don't know.'

'Well I do. You'd probably go under. Unless you could team up with someone else. And chances are, it wouldn't be any better than this. It could be a lot worse.'

'I suppose so,' he conceded.

Greg scooped up a mouthful of water and spat it onto the sand. 'I tell you,' he went on, 'some of them out there are real bad. Like the mob who stopped the car. D'you remember?'

9

He nodded.

'You know what they'd have done to you if I hadn't come along. The same as they did to your old folks.'

Ben stood up abruptly. 'Leave it out, will you!'

'All right. But don't forget that it's me and the gun that've kept you alive so far.'

Ben stared sullenly into the darkness. To his left, low on the horizon, there was a glimmer of lightning. 'It isn't just the gun I'm fed up with,' he said.

'You mean it's me?' Greg's voice was suddenly edgy.

'No, not you either,' he answered truthfully.

'What then?'

He considered the question seriously. 'Myself mainly,' he said at last.

The older boy looked at him, puzzled. 'I reckon you're still a bit high from that thump I gave you. Come on, you'd better get some rest, otherwise you won't be much cop as Caller in the morning.'

He began walking up towards the hut, but Ben remained where he was. 'You'll have to go out on your own tomorrow,' he said.

Greg glanced back. 'How d'you mean?'

'I'm never going to Call again, not for you or anyone.'

'Why not?'

He hesitated. 'Because it's too much like ... like Last Days.'

Greg drew in his breath with a sharp hiss. 'I've told you never to talk about that!' he said angrily. 'Anyway, you're not making sense. Those times are past.'

'I'm still not going to Call.'

Greg laughed humourlessly. 'A couple of days with an empty belly,' he said, 'and you'll change your tune. Now come on.'

Together they trudged back up the slope and re-entered the hut. The fire was still burning and they carefully banked ash around the hot coals, to preserve it until morning. Then, in near darkness, they prepared for sleep – Ben wrapping himself in an old army greatcoat that served as a blanket; Greg, as always, lying down just as he was, the rifle cradled in his arms. Soon there was a sound of deep, regular breathing, only Ben still awake, listening hopefully to the distant growl of thunder. As far as he could judge, it was growing louder, and he tried desperately to remain alert. But he was tired after the events of the day and within minutes he too drifted into sleep.

Almost immediately, it seemed, he was dreaming of the sunlit hillside, observing something he had not actually witnessed – the dingo being clubbed to death. Somehow it was happening without Greg being present. There was just the thud of heavy blows and the dingo looking up at him trustingly. Even in the dream that look was sickeningly familiar. 'No,' he protested, 'don't . . . !' Before he could finish, the dingo's head changed rapidly into something else, and to his horror he found he was gazing down at his own face, the blows falling so fast now, they were like a continuous drum-roll.

With a half-stifled cry he awoke, his face streaming with what he thought at first was sweat. But it was only water leaking in through the bark roof as the whole hut was lashed by rain. This was exactly what he had hoped for, the rain and the noise providing him with the perfect opportunity. He sat up and peered into the darkness.

'Greg?' he said loudly, but his voice was drowned out by the drumming of raindrops and a sustained peal of thunder. Dragging the greatcoat behind him, he crawled across the hut and out into the night. Instantly he was buffeted by wind and rain, and he quickly put on the coat. It was far too big, reaching almost to his heels, but it kept him reasonably dry and warm.

He knew that he didn't have any time to waste. If he was to

11

take full advantage of the storm, which would effectively wipe out any trail he might leave, he had to get well clear of the hut – far enough for Greg to have little chance of picking up his tracks later. The question was, which direction should he choose? Where would Greg be least likely to look for him?

He raised his face to the driving rain, the cold hard drops stinging his flesh and at the same time clearing his mind. It came to him then, where he had to go: the one place he had no desire to revisit; a place Greg would expect him to avoid at all cost.

Even in the pitch darkness he knew the general direction. He barely hesitated. Pulling the wide collar up around his ears, he walked off into the storm.

CHAPTER TWO

He reached the bottom of the final ridge just as dawn was breaking and in the uncertain grey light he laboured up the steep slope. A fine rain was still falling, and the greatcoat, now saturated, dragged on his shoulders like a lead weight, the hem trailing in the mud. But he forced himself to keep moving, making for a tight knot of stringy barks that crowned the ridge. Not until he was hidden in their shadow did he sink to rest.

Below him lay the thin black line of the road. It seemed in reasonable condition, though the normally clear margins on either side were heavily overgrown. To his right was the narrow neck of the valley. A perfect place for an ambush – he could see that now. The burned-out body of the car was still there, its sides streaked with rust. As he should have guessed, it was not the only such wreck: there were others near by, some of them blocking the road entirely; proof that it was no longer in use.

Throughout the long tiring night he had dreaded this moment, fearing that the old memories would start up again, like bad dreams come back to haunt him – his mother's piercing scream as the car door was wrenched open; his father's shouts of protest as figures converged from every side. Never think about Last Days, Greg had warned him repeatedly. And plodding through the rainy night he had struggled to suppress those far-off memories, terrified of what might happen if he acknowledged them. Yet now, faced at last with this place where it had all occurred, he found to his surprise that there was nothing to be particularly frightened of. It was just another stretch of open country, divided in two by the black thread of the road; and the car itself was just another rusted heap blocking the narrow part of the valley.

Confused by his own lack of response, he wondered for a moment whether he had ceased to care. But no, that was not possible, because more than anything else he wished that he could undo the past, make everything the way it had been long ago. So why didn't he now hate this place where so much had ended? Or at least fear it?

The answer came to him quite simply. Because for him nothing had really ended here. It was all still going on. He, acting as a lure day after day, Calling animals to within range of Greg's gun, much as that unknown young man, standing smiling and friendly by the side of the road, had signalled for his father to stop.

Tired, bewildered by his own insights, Ben buried his face in his arms, trying to escape from such thoughts. But in the sudden darkness his father's last words came back with disturbing clarity: 'Run, Ben, run!' That cry somehow becoming confused with the desperate warning he had sent out to the dingo only seconds before the sound of the gun.

Ben stood up and brushed a hand distractedly across his face. In the severe, grey light of dawn, the countryside appeared indescribably gloomy, as though the whole world were in a state of mourning; the sound of the rain, falling softly on the foliage above his head, like a low murmur of grief.

Despite his knowledge that it was dangerous to show himself in daylight, he left the cover of the trees and began running downhill, the sodden greatcoat swishing through the long grass. The burned-out cars lay to his right, and he instinctively avoided them, veering to the left, continuing to run until he reached the thick scrub that bordered the highway. Forcing his way through to the road, he saw, at close quarters, that the tarred surface was in the first stages of breaking up, with weeds and grass flourishing in the widening cracks. But it was still easier to walk on than the ungrazed hillsides, and he followed it automatically, without any clear sense of where he was heading.

As he stumbled on, the day grew lighter, the rain falling about him in a fine misty curtain. There was no one in sight, not even animals, any roos or wallabies having withdrawn into the cover of the tall gums that dotted the landscape. Once this had been good farmland, with a fair sprinkling of wooden farmhouses. Now, most of those he passed were blackened ruins, their brick chimneys pointing upwards like accusing fingers. Only one house within his immediate line of vision was still intact: a low, white-painted cottage set high up the side of the hill, its windows boarded up, a tall barbed-wire fence enclosing it, giving it the appearance of a fortress.

Normally, at the sight of such a place, he would have taken cover; but in his depressed state he didn't bother. With his eyes fixed miserably on the receding line of the road, he walked past in full view of anyone watching from above.

Afterwards, he wasn't sure what had alerted him. The sharp musical call of a magpie, perhaps, making him glance to one side. Whatever the reason, he was in time to see the heavy gates, set in the tall barbed-wire fence, swing open and a horse and rider surge through the gap.

His first impulse was to leave the road and scamper off through the scrub; but in such open country he could never outdistance a man on horseback. His only hope lay in reaching steep or broken terrain where the horse could not follow.

He looked desperately about him. Up ahead the road

15

sloped down towards a concrete-sided bridge that crossed a creek. Downstream, the creek in its periodic floods had badly eroded the valley. He knew that after the heavy rain the whole area would be boggy and unstable, hazardous for a horse. If he could only get there first, he would at least have a chance.

He broke into a run, lumbering along awkwardly in the heavy greatcoat. But already the horseman was threatening to intercept him. Undoing the buttons of the coat, he let it slip off, leaving it where it fell. Glancing around, he saw the horseman change direction. It was exactly the delay Ben needed and he speeded up, running more easily now. By the time the horse forced its way through the scrub at the side of the road, he was well clear, carefully gauging his distance from the bridge, readying himself for the final sprint.

He might just have reached there first if the horse had stopped, but the rider merely leaned sideways in the saddle and scooped the coat up in passing. Then he was urging the horse into a full gallop.

Ben could hear the thud of hoofs as they bit into the soft earth at the edge of the road. He strained forward, committing himself to a pace he could not possibly sustain. And still the hoofbeats were there, growing louder. He looked back once, fleetingly, and saw the fine chestnut head stretched out towards him; the bearded face of the man peering between the flattened ears.

There was, he realized, no hope of evading them. The bridge was too far off. That left only one option. Yet still he hesitated, mindful of a vow he had sworn the previous evening. 'I'm never going to Call again,' he had told Greg. It had been no idle threat, but a solemn promise. And here, already, he was about to break it.

With the taste of defeat in his mouth, he turned and sent out a silent Call. He made it as urgent, as suggestive of danger, as he could, and the horse, never doubting him, attempted to swing away into the scrub. The sudden change

16

of direction caught the rider off balance, but he quickly recovered, sawing savagely at the reins. For a few seconds the horse was pulled two ways at once. As it fought for control, it jittered sideways, up onto the hard black strip of highway which until then the rider had been avoiding. Straight away it lost its footing, its iron-shod hoofs slipping on the unyielding surface, and it crashed to the ground, the rider still in the saddle.

Ben was already backing away as it fell. He expected it to spring up again and gallop off, but it didn't move. Again he Called, and it lifted its head, struggling unsuccessfully to rise. The rider, meanwhile, lay silent and still.

Ben stopped, undecided, the rain like a cool spray upon the flushed skin of his face. He could sense the horse's alarm, feel its deep panic. As he watched, it laid back its ears and whinnied, a high plaintive sound.

'No!' he muttered, guessing already what had to be done – stumbling forward in spite of himself.

His worst fears were soon confirmed: the horse's front legs were unnaturally splayed, one bent sideways at a grotesque angle. The large head drew back as he approached, the eyes showing white with panic.

'It's all right,' he murmured, lulling it with a soothing Call; gently stroking the arch of its neck, his hand brushing away the tiny droplets that clung to the smooth chestnut hair.

It grew rapidly calm, fixing its eyes upon him with that trusting look which he seemed incapable of avoiding. Stepping around the fallen animal, he peered at the rider. He was unconscious, his left leg trapped beneath the heavy body. His right leg hung loosely across the saddle, the booted foot resting on the butt of a rifle. Moving the foot aside, Ben slipped the weapon from its leather sheath. It was similar to Greg's, and he clicked off the safety catch and checked that it was loaded. As he swung the barrel round, the horse, alarmed by the alien smell of the metal, began to toss its head.

17

This time he didn't Call the animal back into a state of calm. Instead, he left it free to calm down gradually, waiting patiently for the wildly tossing head to grow still. Only then did he ease the rifle forward, allowing the end of the barrel to rest gently against the concave shape of the temple. The large honey-coloured eyes looked at him again, without trace of fear. And all at once it seemed to be raining more heavily than ever, drops streaming down his face, blurring his vision. With a quick convulsive movement, he squeezed the trigger.

The recoil jerked the rifle backwards and at the same instant he swivelled round and faced in the opposite direction. Above him, hazy through the grey pall of rain, he could see a line of blue gums, their upper branches ending in delicate tufts of spring growth. Nearer at hand a large apple-gum was in full flower, its yellow blossoms drooping slightly in the rain. Perched on one of the lower limbs was a young currawong, its feathers bedraggled, its powerful beak pointed straight at him.

Ben turned back. The horse was lying peaceful and still, but the rider had regained consciousness and was watching him furtively. There was no trust in that bleak, expectant gaze.

'Go on,' the man said gruffly, 'get it over with.'

Ben wiped the tears from his cheeks. 'What?' he asked, bewildered.

'I said get it over with.'

Ben understood then what he meant. 'You idiot!' he burst out. 'You stupid bloody fool! Don't you ever learn? Doesn't anyone?'

From behind them there came a warning shout. Two figures were running down from the house. The man, still pinned beneath the horse, turned his head, a faint gleam of hope in his eyes.

'About the . . . the horse,' Ben said falteringly. 'I'm sorry. There wasn't anything else to be done.'

Without waiting for a reply, he gathered up the old greatcoat and sprinted for the bridge. He lingered there just long enough to smash the rifle repeatedly against the concrete parapet, putting all his thwarted energy into that act of destruction. Then he slithered down the bank at the far side and ran off along the nearest of the gullies, splashing recklessly through the water and mud.

He hurried on for some time, until he was so tired that he began to stagger. According to his own reckoning, it was mid-morning. The rain had stopped, but the cloud cover persisted. A short distance ahead, set back slightly from the creek, was a cluster of willows, their drooping branches, bright green with fresh growth, reaching to the ground. Once in amongst them he was effectively hidden, and thankfully he sank down on the firm sand, pulling the coat over him as if it were a shell into which he could withdraw.

For a few minutes he lay gazing up at the pattern of branches and young leaves that enclosed him. 'Where am I going?' he wondered.

There was no answer, only a disturbing memory of the horse struggling to rise, its head tossing wildly to and fro. With a determined effort he wiped the image from his mind.

'There must be somewhere!' he muttered. But he was too tired to think, and regretfully he closed his eyes.

As always, he fell into a vivid sequence of dreams, though for once they lacked any nightmarish quality. In place of the usual dark images, he dreamed simply of his former life in Sydney; of the carefree existence he had shared with his parents in their small house in Coogee. Nothing very much happened in the dreams, but they were filled with light and air and a feeling of peace.

When he awoke, late afternoon sunshine was streaming down through the tree. The sun and the breeze had almost dried the greatcoat, and if it hadn't been for the hollow ache in his stomach he would have felt comfortable. As sometimes happens at the moment of waking, he was not conscious of what he had dreamed and he was vaguely puzzled by a lingering sense of contentment. Pushing aside the coat, he stole down to the creek, hoping that if he drank enough water he would drive away some of the dull hunger-ache.

It was as he was straightening up from the stream that his dreams came rushing back in all their vividness – the restful atmosphere of the house; the murmur of familiar voices; his own room, filled with the soft pulsing sound of the sea. He knew those times were gone, never to return. But it occurred to him that the house would still be there. So why not return? Sydney couldn't be all that far away. And would the city be any more hopeless than the bush? At least there would be no animals roaming the deserted streets, waiting to be Called.

He stood up and turned towards the east, the setting sun casting his own shadow upon the path he must take. 'Maybe I'll go home,' he murmured aloud.

As he did so he detected something. It was very faint, coming from far beyond the horizon, an answer to a Call he had never consciously made. He listened hard and it came again: the wordless response of a mind so defiant, so savagely distrustful and unforgiving, that he felt momentarily awed. And also strangely compelled, drawn by its mingled suggestion of danger and promise.

CHAPTER THREE

He found the main road quite easily and followed it all that night. Now that no cars travelled the highway, it was as safe as anywhere, the roadblocks having long been abandoned. Occasionally he startled wallabies or roos that had been attracted by the warmth of the tarred surface, but he was never tempted to Call them. At other times, when the night was especially silent, he listened for the awesome response he had detected earlier. Although he didn't hear it again, he continued to sense that something was out there, a great distance off, some savage intelligence luring him on.

At the first sign of grey light he left the road. He was tired by then, but also very hungry, and he decided to push on for a while, taking advantage of whatever cover he could find. Further to the south there was a narrow belt of trees, and he reached this just as day was breaking.

Tired though he was, he realized that somehow he had to find food. The question was how to go about it. He was still puzzling over this problem when he came to an untidy heap of grey boulders that interrupted the belt of trees – exactly the kind of place where snakes and lizards were likely to take refuge. With the sun already risen, all he had to do was wait for its warmth to tempt them out.

Armed with a stick, he crouched at the edge of the clearing

and watched. Minutes later, a fat-bodied shingleback lumbered out onto a slab of sunlit rock. Leaping to his feet, Ben scrambled after it. But there was no need for haste: still cold and sluggish, it could do no more than raise its head and display, its mouth gaping wide, hissing at him; and quickly he swung the stick, hitting it several times, until it lay limp and still.

In spite of his experience with Greg, the act of killing sickened him. Reluctantly he picked up the scaly body. It was half a metre long and thicker than his own arm, but he had no knife to cut it up with, nor any means of cooking it. What was he supposed to do, he wondered, tear it open with his teeth? Devour the raw flesh? He knew that when he was hungry enough he would do precisely that. But he hadn't reached that point yet.

There were some smaller stones at the base of the rock-pile and he smashed these together. With the more jagged splinters he managed to hack open the shingleback's soft belly-skin. Once he had cleaned the carcass, he wrapped it in leaves and rolled it tightly in his coat, to protect it from flies.

'For later,' he told himself vaguely. And with that grisly thought he lay down in the nearest shade and slept.

A little past the middle of the afternoon he awoke to the smell of burning. Grey smoke was drifting through the trees and he suspected at first that he was in the path of a bush fire. But the bush was still damp from the recent rain; and there was no floating ash or soot in the air about him. Puzzled, he tucked the rolled-up coat under his arm and made his way to the edge of the trees. Peering through the long grass, he saw it: a house on the far side of the paddock, smoke curling up from what remained of its walls and roof. The fire must have been started hours earlier, because now there was no one in sight, and the house and most of its out-buildings were all but gutted.

For nearly an hour Ben stayed where he was, watching. He

would have preferred to wait until darkness, but he needed the fire and he was worried that it might go out. At last, reasonably satisfied, he ran, bent over, through the long grass, stopping periodically to check his surroundings.

He reached the dirt road bordering the house and again took cover, making a final check. The scene before him was not unfamiliar: the tall protective fence smashed down; the vegetable garden trampled; the buildings looted and burned. Two bodies, of a man and a woman, were lying stretched out beneath a pepper tree that had once shaded the verandah. Even from where he crouched, Ben could tell they were beyond his help.

Cautiously, he stood up and approached the smoking ruins. But while he was still crossing the trampled garden, something stirred beside the dead body of the woman. It was a small cattle-dog: its fur had been singed almost to the colour of ashes, but it was still defiant, its lips drawn back in a warning snarl.

Ben held out a hand enticingly. 'Come on, boy,' he crooned, 'it's all over now.'

The dog eyed him suspiciously and growled another warning.

'I'm not going to hurt you,' Ben murmured.

He took a step forward, and the animal started to bark.

'Hush!' Ben said urgently. 'Be quiet!'

His voice only excited the animal further and it danced towards him, barking more shrilly. Ben glanced nervously around, aware that if anybody were still in the vicinity this kind of noise would soon attract them. Which meant that he had to act fast.

Clutching the carcass of the shingleback to his chest, he eyed the smouldering remains of the house longingly. Once again something Greg had said came back to him: 'A couple of days with an empty belly and you'll change your tune.' A couple of days! That was all it had taken! Even less, because there had been the episode with the horse. No, he thought defensively, that was different . . . and so is this. But even as he gave in to his hunger and silently Called to the dog, he secretly admitted that this too was just another betrayal of his earlier promise.

The dog had stopped barking and was watching him uncertainly. It was too late for Ben to retreat and he repeated the Call. The small animal immediately abandoned all show of resistance: with its tail wagging, its belly brushing the ground, it crept towards him, whimpering softly. Ben fondled its head, not daring to look into its eyes for fear of what he would find there, and hurried towards the ruins of the house.

He thought he would have to rake away the ash and search for the remains of the live coals, but quite by chance everything had been prepared for him. The roof had been the last part of the house to cave in, and the sheets of unpainted corrugated iron were burning hot, like a ready-made barbecue. All he had to do was unwrap the carcass and place it directly on the hot surface.

While he was waiting for the lizard to cook, he explored the area around the house. Almost everything of any use had been stolen or destroyed. The only objects still intact were the water tank and an old corrugated-iron shed near the back fence. The door of the shed had been torn off and the interior was strewn with debris. Left to himself, Ben would probably not have lingered in there, but the dog began scratching at the earth floor.

'What is it, boy?' Ben asked sharply.

The dog continued with its scratching, and Ben crouched down to inspect the floor for himself. Beneath a layer of dust was a dull glint of metal. It gave off a hollow ring when he rapped it, and with a start of recognition he guessed what he had found. Eagerly, he too began scrabbling in the dust, but before he could investigate further he caught the tantalizing scent of grilled meat and ran back to the house.

For a while he was too busy satisfying his hunger to think of anything else. Not until he had picked the bones clean and had a long drink from the tank did he return to the shed.

As he suspected, he had stumbled on a hidden cellar. When he cleared away the earth and pulled the sheet of steel aside, he found a ladder leading down into darkness, a torch hanging in readiness from the top rung. With the light to guide him, he descended the ladder, leaving the dog whining nervously at the top.

He found himself in a room with rough earth walls and timber supports. It contained everything necessary for survival: stacks of dried and tinned food; cannisters of water; blankets, kerosene, tools – even two bicycles, equipped with heavy-duty tyres in case it was ever necessary to escape along the back roads. So why hadn't the owners of the house escaped, or at least hidden in this room? Had the attack been too sudden? Or had they somehow been tricked, much as his parents had been tricked perhaps, by a friendly face they believed they could trust? Trust! The word alone was enough to make him flinch guiltily, and he climbed hastily back up the ladder.

The sun was low in the sky when he emerged from the shed and he crouched thoughtfully in the lengthening shadows. Finding the storeroom had been a marvellous piece of luck. What he had to decide was how to use that luck. Should he stay here and live off the supplies? It was the sensible thing to do. There was enough food to last him for months. And he would be reasonably safe: soon this would be just another burned-out property, of no more interest than any other.

After two days with an empty stomach, the idea of a regular food supply was particularly attractive. Yet still he hesitated. If you stay put, Greg had insisted, you're a sitting duck – sooner or later someone'll spot you, and then . . . zap! And even if that didn't happen, what would he do when the food

25

was used up? Wouldn't it be better to take this opportunity to escape? To stick to his half-formulated plan of heading for Sydney?

He stood up, undecided. Before him, the yellow ball of the sun slipped towards the horizon. As it hung there, in the dying moments of the day, he heard again the same far-off response he had detected on the previous evening. But slightly clearer now: a passionate expression of freedom; the brief outburst of a mind that recognizes neither fear nor dependence. He heard it only once, but that soundless cry, terrible and challenging, was enough to decide him.

In the waning dusk he began preparing for the journey ahead. First he hoisted one of the bicycles up through the trapdoor. It was equipped with a back carrier, and onto this he tied a rucksack which he filled with tinned food. Apart from the food he took little else – some matches, a sheath knife, a canvas water bag, and a pair of binoculars. None of the clothing fitted him and so he kept the old army greatcoat, tying it across the handlebars.

It was nearly dark by the time he had finished and he was impatient to set off. But he felt he owed the people of the house something. Taking a spade from the underground room, he dug a shallow grave and rolled the two bodies into it, covering the mound with a piece of roofing iron, to protect it from dingoes.

With that last duty completed, and with the underground room again concealed, he wheeled the bicycle over to the road. The night was cool and dark, and as he settled himself in the saddle he was filled with a strange excitement, as if he were being given a second chance, an opportunity to wipe out the mistakes of the past.

He began pedalling down the road, so engrossed by his own thoughts that he had gone some distance before he became aware of the dog loping along beside him. He stopped and

26

looked down. 'No, not you,' he said regretfully. 'Stay here, where you belong.'

It whimpered and moved closer to the bicycle. There was one sure way of sending it back, but he balked at that. And it crossed his mind that the dog could, after all, be useful: its keen senses would be an added protection on the road. 'All right,' he said, relenting, 'you can stick around for a while.'

Not for some days did he come to regret that decision and to realize that he had fallen into the same old trap yet again.

CHAPTER FOUR

Now that he had committed himself to returning to Sydney, he pressed on as hard as he could, travelling at night and resting by day. Despite the weight of the rucksack, he found that cycling was less tiring than walking. Also he enjoyed it more: the rapid, even motion; the rush of cool air against his face. Most of all he liked free-wheeling down the long hills. As the bicycle picked up speed he would click his tongue and the dog would leap up onto the coat draped across the handlebars. Leaning forward, his cheek pressed against the dog's quivering side, he would go hurtling down through the darkness, the bicycle bouncing over the splits in the tarred surface.

In a very different way he also enjoyed the days – their calm, uneventful quality. Holed up in some ruined house or hidden in a clump of trees, he was able to sleep more peacefully than he had for months. Always, when he awoke in the late afternoon, the dog would be sitting there watching over him, its eyes bright with expectation; and the moment he stretched and yawned, it would leap up, eager for the journey ahead.

'It's all right for you,' Ben would grumble as he climbed stiffly to his feet, 'you're not weighed down by a load of gear.' But secretly he was growing fond of the small animal, even though, wary as ever, he refused to give it a name.

That first part of the journey was generally a carefree time for both of them. The one moment of danger occurred early on, when Ben foolishly tried to cycle through a small town. He noticed the old sixty-kilometre sign at the town's edge, its pole bent, the sign itself peppered with shot, but he decided to push on anyway. It was only the dog which saved him. Long before he heard a sound, it growled out a low warning. Ben stopped and listened. From somewhere ahead there came a shuffling noise, of someone creeping towards him. Quietly, he wheeled the bicycle off the road and into the overgrown ditch, he and the dog crouching behind a cluster of young wattles. Minutes later, by the meagre light of a thin moon, he saw the tall figure of a man emerge from the shadows.

'See anything?' a voice hissed.

The man stopped and peered along the dark road. Ben, now lying flat on the ground, was so close he could hear his wheezing breath.

'No,' the man answered gruffly, 'musta bin a roo or somethin'.'

He turned and shuffled back to his hiding place, speaking loudly to his companion. And Ben, under cover of their voices, picked up the bicycle and stole off.

It had been a narrow escape, and from then on he gave any settlement a wide berth. He was especially careful to avoid the bigger towns – now dark, deserted clusters of dwellings – circling around them in the dead of night; always moving steadily eastwards, drawing closer to the Great Dividing Range.

As he travelled, he grew more confident that he was not just running away. Pedalling laboriously up the foothills of the mountains, he felt that the past was over and done with; that he was making a wholly fresh start. Admittedly there had been that episode with the horse, but that too lay behind him. From now on, he told himself, there would be no more

29

broken trust. Life in Sydney, somehow, would be different.

He was encouraged in that belief by the strange, defiant cry which originated somewhere beyond the mountains. It reached out to him every evening, just as darkness was about to descend. Day by day it grew louder, and he was almost sure now that it issued from some kind of animal. Why such an animal should be living in suburban Sydney he had no idea; but he never doubted that it was there, a creature different from any animal he had encountered in the bush. And from that alone he took courage, interpreting it as a sign, a proof of the new life that awaited him.

With the end of his journey now so close, he decided as an added precaution not to follow the main road over the Blue Mountains, but rather to take the old Aboriginal route, known as the Bells Line of Road. As he had hoped, it was deserted, its surface eroded by rain and frost. He crossed the heights in the middle of the night, the stars so bright in the chill atmosphere that he felt he could brush them with his fingertips. Wrapped warmly in the greatcoat, the dog perched precariously on the handlebars, he breathed in the cool air and just caught the distant, musty odour of the forested valleys, the scent blown to him on the night wind. 'Soon,' he murmured happily, 'soon,' feeling the bicycle gather speed as he began the long descent.

When dawn broke he was still in the hills, though not far above the river which separated the mountains from the plains. He would have liked to push on, but he was passing houses now, at fairly regular intervals, most of them ruined or deserted, and he decided not to take unnecessary risks. Half way down a steep, thickly forested section of the road, he ran the bicycle in amongst the trees and stopped for the day.

The sun rose soon afterwards. And while he was still eating a simple meal, the bell-birds began calling, their clear melodious song filling the morning. There was something so joyous, so untroubled about their song that it was hard to believe that the previous two years had ever occurred. Everything, it seemed, was back to normal. He, too, returning to where he truly belonged. The nightmare over at last.

With that thought he curled up on the soft leaf-mould and went peacefully to sleep. Only the dog remained wakeful: its light brown eyes, formerly so trusting, now watchful and alert; its sharp kelpie snout pointing uneasily towards the plains.

He slept longer than usual, until after sunset, and so he failed to detect that defiant cry which always greeted the night. It was the dog, whining nervously, which finally roused him and he sat up in the dusky light and stretched lazily.

'Not far to go now,' he said, failing to notice that the dog was restless and edgy.

Swallowing a hasty meal, he wheeled the bicycle out onto the road. Already he could smell the muddy dampness of the river. Silently, with only the faint swish of the tyres to mark his progress, he allowed the natural slope of the road to draw him downwards, the dog crouched before him as he steered around the shadowy bends.

The moon had risen when he reached the river. By its dim light he could just make out the whitish outline of the bridge, the twin lanes choked with burned-out cars. It was the kind of scene he had expected, a typical remnant of Last Days, and he stopped briefly. Half-hidden by the scrub at the road's edge, he surveyed the clogged, narrow crossing.

'What d'you think?' he murmured, addressing the dog as if it were another human being.

The animal tensed forward, listening, scenting the breeze. What little wind there was blew fitfully down river, carrying with it the odour of mud and rotting vegetation. Apart from the doleful call of a mo-poke and the murmurings of the river itself, the night was silent.

'Looks pretty safe to me,' Ben whispered – and when the

31

dog failed to growl a definite warning, he cycled cautiously into the open.

It was not easy crossing the bridge. The jumble of car bodies blocked not only the road, but also the raised pedestrian area on one side. Wherever possible Ben wove a path between the rusting hulks. In the very worst places he had to lift the bicycle onto his shoulders and clamber unsteadily over the crumpled wrecks. Even so, he took care not to make a sound – which was why, when he reached the far side, he was not caught unawares.

Once again it was the dog that alerted him. As it let out its familiar low growl, Ben froze into stillness. Hardly daring to breathe, he peered into the darkness. The way ahead seemed clear at first; then there was a movement in the shadows and he saw a man pace slowly out into the middle of the road and stop. He was facing away from the bridge, a short thick-set figure, a gun held loosely in one hand.

The dog was already edging away; but for Ben there was no going back. The bridge, strewn with its grim reminders of betrayal and violence, was too like the past he was fleeing from. There was only one way for him to go now: forward, towards the city; to the house he had grown up in, its rooms filled with the echo of memories he could happily live with.

As if sensitive to his secret feelings, the dog moved up beside him. It too had abandoned any thoughts of retreat, its hackles raised, its lips drawn back in a silent snarl. There was no need for Ben to issue a command. He had only to touch the animal's shoulder and it darted along the road, its teeth sinking into the back of the man's thigh. At the same instant Ben bore down on the pedals, surging out into the open.

Confused by the suddenness of the attack, the man spun around, flailing at the dog. Just for a moment, in the silvered darkness, Ben saw his ravaged face tilted up in astonishment. Then, using the weight and momentum of the bicycle, he shouldered the man aside and sped off. Behind him he heard

32

a shouted curse followed by a sharp explosion, and seconds later the dog was scuttling along beside him, barking excitedly.

He didn't silence it straight away. He was too excited himself for that. Like the unknown beast that called to him each evening, he felt suddenly free, defiant. The cool night wind seemed to be sweeping the past two years away for ever, and it occurred to him that in crossing the river he had accomplished the most difficult part of his journey.

'Good boy,' he called encouragingly, 'well done.' And the dog, responding to his voice, leaped onto the handlebars and licked eagerly at his face.

They were still in that happy frame of mind when they entered the outlying towns of Richmond and Windsor. Ben had formed a clear idea of what they would be like: deserted and overgrown, but otherwise unspoiled; the buildings and fences largely intact; the main road lined with empty red-roofed cottages. What he found made his heart sink, the towns themselves more like places in one of his nightmares: the fences trampled down; the houses vandalized, their walls blackened by fire, their doors and windows smashed; the broken remains of furniture strewn across the concrete driveways. And with wrecked cars everywhere, like great metal beasts wallowing in the head-high scrub that flourished along the roadside.

Nor were the towns completely deserted. More than once he saw human shapes slink away through the scrub; and at one point, where the road was almost blocked by a fallen power pole, the ragged figure of a man ran out and attacked him. It was only the dog, worrying at the man's heels, which enabled him to slip past, a hoarse cry of animal rage following him as he pedalled off.

Once clear of Windsor, he tried telling himself that things would improve as he drew nearer to Sydney – that the outlying towns were so dangerous because of the influence of

33

the bush. But it didn't take him long to realize his error. As he passed through one built-up area after another, the nightmare only grew worse. More and more frequently he was waylaid, wild figures leaping out of the scrub, rocks and sticks whistling past his head, howls of anger disrupting the stillness of the night.

He soon learned that his best chance of survival lay in silence and speed, and he hunched over the handlebars and began pedalling with frantic energy. Shadowy figures continued to leap out, some of them armed with rifles or weighted sticks; but with the dog snapping at their heels they were always too late to intercept him, and he would sweep past to be swallowed again by the darkness.

Eventually it wasn't these half-wild human beings who stopped him, but rather the nervous strain of travelling through this lightless region of violence and despair. And shortly before midnight he paused to rest. He had just encountered a crude road-block and had swung aside into a maze of side streets. It was while he was trying to find his way back to the main road that he simply gave up and took refuge in one of the ruined houses, where he crouched, wakeful and tense, for the remainder of the night.

By dawn he felt not only tired, but dispirited and close to defeat. As the light strengthened, he looked about him at his place of refuge. It was a shattered husk of a house: the blackened walls cracked and leaning at crazy angles; the roof half fallen-in; the floorboards already spongy to the touch and beginning to rot. Even at their worst, he and Greg had never lived in such a place. Yet during the night he had clung to this ruin. Now, with the early morning sunlight streaming through the shattered windows, he recognized why. He hadn't merely been afraid of those darkened streets. His real fear had been of what he might find if he pressed on and succeeded in reaching his former home. This perhaps? Or less? A few crumbling walls fronting onto the endless sea.

He shuddered at the prospect. But equally he knew that to cycle on was no more dangerous than to turn back. Also, having begun this journey, he felt a strange impulse to see it through to its end, whatever the outcome.

His one real regret was for the dog sleeping peacefully in the corner, its nose tucked against its side. This was no place for it, this shattered remnant of a city. He should have left it back there in the bush. He had only brought it with him to ensure his own safety. The tireless brown body, the trusting and alert mind, both used by him. The same old story all over again. A story which, for the dog anyway, could have only one ending, somewhere out there on the road during the coming night. He didn't know precisely when or how it would happen, but he could guess – picturing to himself that moment when he would have to choose between his own survival and the dog's. And with a murmur of shame and regret, he crawled to the farthest corner of the room and lay down alone to sleep.

CHAPTER FIVE

The sun had set and he was standing just inside the shattered doorway, ready to leave. His thoughts were so fixed upon the journey ahead that he had forgotten about the wordless cry which always rang through his mind at dusk, and when it came it caught him by surprise. It was clearer than ever now and nothing like the shouts and screams that had followed him during the previous night. There had been more than a suggestion of madness about those shouts; whereas this cry, for all its power and savagery, contained none of that crazed, vicious quality. In the brooding dusk it was more like an expression of sanity; the outpouring of a mind that was defiant and untrusting, that would crush anything that stood in its way, but was yet balanced, confident of its strength and purpose.

Although he still found it awesome, it was for Ben a truly welcome sound because it proved that at least one creature had managed to resist the destructive pressures of this terrible city. That thought alone was enough to restore his courage, giving point to his journey, so that when he wheeled the bicycle out onto the unlit street he did so with none of the dread he had anticipated. Despite all that had happened, he knew it was still possible that a place of sanctuary persisted at the heart of the city – like a sunlit island in the midst of turbulent waters.

Without that hope to buoy him up, it is doubtful whether he could have survived the night that followed. As he penetrated deeper and deeper into what was left of suburban Sydney, the atmosphere of madness grew ever stronger. Hysterical voices, more bird-like than human, screeched at him as he passed; thin wasted figures, dressed in a weird variety of looted clothing, hobbled after him, cursing or pleading with him to stop. Most of them were too weak, too overcome by despair, to cause him any serious problem and he soon left them behind. But there were others, young men and women often not much older than himself, who lunged at him with a far more deadly intent. Lithe and sinister, armed with clubs or knives or even guns, they brought home to him the reality of what he was doing – running a perilous gauntlet, with no guarantee of safety at the end.

Again and again in the course of the night he was saved from disaster only by the keen senses and courageous actions of the dog. It alerted him to road-blocks and ambushes; and, at times of particular danger, it hurled itself at their attackers, giving Ben the chance to slip away. After one of his more narrow escapes, as he was sprinting down a lonely side street, he glanced at the dog running beside him and noticed that it was limping. At the first opportunity he stopped and inspected the small animal. The moon was not bright enough for him to see clearly, but when he ran his hands along the close fur of the dog's side, it yelped plaintively and his fingers came away moist and black in the dim moonlight.

'Come,' he whispered gently, patting the coat draped across the handlebars. But the dog, previously so full of energy, lacked the strength to spring up in one bound and had to scramble its way onto the coat.

He kept mainly to the side streets after that, stopping frequently to listen, using the stars to guide him. Earlier in the evening he had hoped to cross the Parramatta River and enter the southerly portion of the city from the west, but after the first few detours he had become hopelessly lost in the north-western suburbs. He suspected now that he was heading for the harbour, which he would somehow have to cross, but with the dog injured it was too late to backtrack and he plunged on recklessly.

Even moving far more slowly and furtively, skulking along the scrub-lined minor roads, still he occasionally ran into trouble. Pathetic, emaciated creatures, the scarecrow remains of human beings, would start up before him, their faces disfigured by malice or fear, their meagre bodies materializing out of the shadows. And in spite of its injury the dog would leap to his defence, snapping and tearing at the ragged legs and bare feet, clearing the road ahead.

Always, after one of these encounters, its limp was more pronounced, its brave attempt to jump up onto the handlebars less successful than before. Until at last, in the early hours of the morning, it became so weak that it could barely catch up with the bicycle, and as it ran it left a thin wet trickle on the dark surface of the road. Ben scooped it up in his arms and held the small quivering body against his chest.

'That's enough,' he murmured, looking around for a house in which to hide.

But by then he had reached an entirely different part of the city, with a wholly new feel about it. The street in which he was standing was overlooked by tall commercial buildings and there was a changed quality in the air, a strangeness that he could not identify at first. He took a deep breath – and suddenly realized he could smell the sea. As he recognized its familiar scent, all the old associations of home and happiness came rushing in upon him, and for a moment he had to fight off an irrational impulse to burst into tears.

'We're going to make it!' he assured the dog in a broken whisper. 'I promise you, we'll get there!'

Settling the dog comfortably between his arms, he pedalled

along the street, keeping to the deep shadow of the buildings. At the first intersection he stopped and peered around the corner. He found himself staring along a multi-lane highway. Like most such highways it was littered with rusting car bodies. Yet it wasn't these which now made him catch his breath: rather it was what lay at the end of the long clean curve of this particular road. For there, not far away, etched against the dark sky and the distant high-rise buildings, was the unmistakable shape of Sydney Harbour Bridge.

'I told you!' he whispered joyously, clutching the dog towards him. 'Didn't I say we'd get here?'

The bridge itself was not his ultimate destination, but seeing it there, unchanged, like a welcome vision from the past, gave him new heart. Once on the other side, he would be only a short ride from home and in territory he knew like the back of his hand. The one remaining problem was how to reach that far shore. And at the thought of actually crossing the bridge, he grew instantly sober.

The sensible course of action, he suspected, would be to hide somewhere within sight of the bridge in order to spy out the land during the coming day. That way, he would be well rested and reasonably sure of what he was up against when he came to attempt the crossing. The trouble with that scheme, however, was the strain it would place upon both his own patience and the waning strength of the dog. He was by no means certain that his nerve would hold for another twenty-four hours; and he had no idea whether the dog would still be fit to travel. No, far better to face the risks and dangers now.

In the cover of the nearest doorway he made a few simple preparations. After a brief check of the ropes binding the rucksack to the carrier, he hung the binoculars and half-empty water bottle about his neck. Then, placing the injured animal on the handlebars, he pushed the bicycle out onto the road and swung into the saddle.

He didn't sprint at first – he was content to conserve his

energy, pedalling steadily, looking warily about him. Nothing stirred out there on the open road, no flickering shadows moving between the wrecked cars, and gradually he increased his pace. As he came round the final part of the gently curving bend, he worked up to top speed, committing himself to the crossing. Ahead of him, the tall concrete structures of the bridge loomed into view, the great sections of steel arching away. With the tyres humming on the smooth surface, he made a final effort, intent on the long straight highway which seemed to broaden and open before him.

'Here we go!' he whispered excitedly.

But the dog, suddenly stiffening between his arms, threw back its head and began to bark. And seconds later, as he sped through the old toll gates, dark figures swarmed out onto the road in front of him. There was no time to make conscious decisions. Clenching both handbrakes full on, he brought the bicycle round in a great broadside. His initial speed carried him smoothly into the long dangerous slide; but as he lost momentum and the tyres began to grip, the machine seemed to come alive, bucking beneath him. He felt the dog slip from between his arms; and then he was thrown clear, rolling over and over; glimpsing, as he turned, the way the bicycle tore a gap in the line of waiting figures.

He was up immediately, scrambling for the gap and the wide, shadowy spaces of the bridge beyond.

'Get him, Chas!' someone shouted.

One of the attackers, short and powerful, most of his face masked by a balaclava, lunged towards him. He dodged, tore the binoculars from around his neck and swung them by the strap, forcing the masked head away and back. Another figure, eyes shadowed by a peaked cap, the rest of the face thin and ratlike, ran forward, but this time it was the dog that intervened. Growling and snapping, it leaped straight at the man's chest, tearing at his throat.

'Chas!' the voice screamed.

Ben was through the gap in the line, but from the bridge ahead more figures appeared, running. He hesitated and the others circled quickly about him, forcing him back against the barrier that separated the traffic lanes from the old public walkway on the easterly side of the bridge. Only the dog, bristling and growling, stood between him and his attackers.

Ben knew that if he held his ground he would have no chance. Equally, if he and the dog vaulted the barrier and tried to run for it, they would soon be hunted down. What he needed was time. Delay. An opportunity to outdistance his pursuers. And that could only be achieved if he was prepared ... if he ...

He drew in a slow sobbing breath. He remembered that somewhere a long time ago – or had it been recently? he wasn't sure any longer – he had foreseen this situation, this kind of choice. Between his own safety and a question of trust, fidelity. With only one possible outcome. Always the same one where he was concerned. Always.

He wiped his hand across his mouth, as though trying to scrub away some foul taint that clung to his lips; but it remained there, like a bitter potion that refused to be removed.

'Stay!' he said aloud, mouthing the word rather than silently Calling to the animal – as if that alone made it any less of a betrayal. But the dog merely looked back questioningly, confused by the sound, allowing the attackers to creep forward, the half-circle to tighten.

'Steady now,' a voice said, the words coming from the man in the balaclava, 'make sure you get the little bastard this time.'

Ben could hear their combined breaths, hoarse, straining, as they prepared to rush in. And quickly, while he still had the chance, he averted his eyes from the injured dog and Called the one brief command that was necessary. Then, still with his face turned away, he clambered swiftly over the barrier

41

and began to run along the walkway.

Behind him he could hear shouts and snarls as the dog held the men at bay. He wanted to Call again, to beckon to the dog this time, but he lacked the courage. A flight of stone steps appeared before him and he ran down them, aware as he did so of a long high-pitched scream somewhere in the background. He couldn't tell at first whether it came from the dog or one of the men; but as he reached the bottom of the steps and ran out into the deserted street, not only the scream, but all noise of the fight died away abruptly. And he knew then what that final cry had meant.

He stopped only for a few seconds and stared miserably about him, as though searching for something. For what? A name . . . ? Yes, that was it, a name. But he hadn't given it one! Rufusing it even that simple recognition, that most basic of dignities. Acting, all along, as if it had no identity. None!

He began running again, his solitary footsteps echoing through the darkness. Somewhere, far off, a wailing voice was calling out, repeating a single word over and over again: 'Dog . . . dog . . . dog . . . dog . . . !'

There was no answering bark, only the echo of other footsteps as someone leapt down the steps after him. He could see, a short distance ahead, a narrow alleyway set between an old red-brick building and the curving ramparts of a traffic lane that fed onto the bridge. He darted down it and emerged at the edge of a small park. Whimpering now, half-blinded by tears, he ran through the tall stringy grass, his shadow passing smoothly beneath the trees, down towards a bordering strip of suburban garden. Left untended, the garden had become a miniature wilderness. Groping his way past frangipani trees and weeping tendrils of bougainvillaea, he finally came to a halt. Only metres from where he stood was a dense cluster of hibiscus bushes and he burrowed in amongst them and lay still.

Out on the street he could hear voices calling to each other.

But it was another noise, nearer at hand, which bothered him: his own whimpering, a hopeless animal sound that he was powerless to stop. The voices drew closer, heavy figures blundering through the park, and still the whimpering went on, even though he covered his mouth and nose with both hands and buried his head in the leaves and rank grass.

'Hey, Chas!' someone called. 'Listen!'

There was a momentary silence, disturbed only by his muffled cries.

'What d'you reckon?'

'Dunno. Could be that dog.'

'I thought we finished it off.'

'So did I.'

'Shall we go after it?'

'No, waste of time. It's the kid I want. Did you see him run? Like a bloody deer! He's the one, I tell you.'

The figures crashed away through the undergrowth, leaving him alone. Gradually the plaintive animal sounds, issuing involuntarily from his mouth and throat, died down, the moon-silvered night slipping back into stillness. He stood up, his face grimy and tear-stained. The strap of the binoculars was still twined about his fingers, but the binoculars themselves had disappeared, as had the canvas water bag. He shrugged indifferently. What did it matter? With his journey and all his hopes for the future reduced to this: a ruined garden in the midst of a city run mad, the heavy silence haunted by the scream of a dying animal. After that, what did anything matter?

Yet still he couldn't remain where he was. It occurred to him that he had to do something, go somewhere; and out of habit his mind turned again to the idea of the house in Coogee. To reach it he had to cross the harbour, but the bridge now was out of the question. That left one alternative: to work his way along the shoreline in the hope of finding an old boat.

With dragging steps he left the garden and plodded wearily through the streets of Kirribilli, heading for the harbour. He soon found the boats he was looking for, but like the cars on the highways they were wrecks, a shattered collection of hulls littering the shoreline. He stood amongst the wreckage, staring bleakly across the wind-ruffled water at the Opera House and the tall blank shapes of the high-rise buildings. He had lost all desire to go on and it was only the forbidding structure of the bridge, looming up on his right, which prompted him to turn and stumble off towards the east.

He made no attempt to hide now, walking openly through the streets, cutting back periodically in order to stay close to the water. Yet never once was he challenged, only the pale moon, low in the sky, gazing down at him. There was a feeling in the air which told him it was morning, but beyond that he had very little sense of time. So that when dawn did begin to break, it caught him unprepared.

He had again strayed from the harbour and he decided to cut back once more, his course leading him to an area of parkland flanked by surprisingly heavy bush – the park itself fronting onto a small, curved beach. Just out from the beach, in the shallow water, an old-fashioned fishing launch was lying on its side. From where he stood, he couldn't tell whether or not it was intact and he stumbled down to the beach and waded out through the shallows, the water striking cold on his bare legs. As soon as he climbed aboard and dropped down through the hatch, he realized that the old craft was useless for his purposes: she had been holed and water was slopping around inside. Still, she was fairly dry up near the bows, and with full dawn about to break this seemed as good a place as any to spend the day.

He groped his way to the forward bunk and lay down, but tired though he was, sleep felt a long way off. Close to where he lay, small waves slapped monotonously against the damaged hull; while in the background the waning night

44

continued to be disturbed by animal cries, as if the dog were still calling to him. Several minutes passed before he realized that those cries originated not in his own troubled mind, but outside.

Vaguely curious, he forced open the forward hatch and stared out. The bush-covered eastern shore, curving around to a distant headland, showed as a thick dark smudge, the sky lightening above. From within that uncertain darkness came a random series of grunts and calls, most of them foreign to him, totally out of place in that setting. Unless ... unless ... In a flood of understanding he recognized where he was. Close to Taronga Park Zoo! With the animals somehow still inside, surviving in the midst of all this chaos! He didn't know how that was possible, yet he had no doubt that they were in there. Alive, calling to him.

He hoisted himself up onto the edge of the hatchway, everything suddenly clear at last. Yes, this was the source of that savage cry which had reached across the horizon each evening, luring him on night after night. This the true end of his journey all along, the one place he was fated to come to. But why here? And why him in particular? The answer, like the dawn, seemed to dissolve the surrounding darkness, leaving him sitting out in the open, exposed by the strengthening light. He slipped quickly back into the dim interior of the launch, but even as he crouched on the damp bunk he suspected that it was no use hiding. Having travelled so far to reach this place, he knew, as by instinct, that he would not easily avoid what was awaiting him here. An ordeal of some kind – he was sure of that. A trial or test that might well find him wanting.

PART II

THE TRIAL

CHAPTER SIX

It was thirst which drove him from the boat. In the middle of the afternoon, too parched to sleep, he slipped quietly over the side and waded ashore, intending to search for water. As far as he could tell there was no one about, the overgrown park warm and still in the bright sunlight. But no sooner was he clear of the beach, pushing his way through the tall grass, than he heard a quick light tread and, before he could turn, an arm encircled his neck and he was dragged backwards.

'Got you!' a voice whispered, the words breathed into his ear.

Oddly, in the first moment of capture, he experienced neither terror nor disappointment. If anything, he felt only a mild sense of relief, that this should have happened at last, removing the burden of what to do next.

'You're choking me!' he gasped.

The pressure on his throat eased and the arm withdrew, replaced instantly by the cool touch of a knife blade on the side of his neck. Instinctively, he tried to pull away, but the knife followed him, nicking his flesh so that a drop of blood ran down onto his chest.

'You got the message?' the voice asked quietly.

He nodded and caught a glimpse, at the very edge of his vision, of a thin undernourished face, identical to one he had encountered on the bridge the night before, the features sharp and ratlike.

'You sure about that?' The pressure of the knife increased slightly.

'No, don't . . . please . . .' he stammered, acting out the same cringing role he had always used with Greg.

'That's better,' the voice murmured, gratified. 'Now let's have some introductions. Name of Trev. And you?'

'Ben.'

'Right, Ben. Time for a little walk.'

Guided by a hand that grasped him by the scruff of the neck, he stumbled forward, soon crossing the parkland and emerging into a series of steep, overgrown streets. Here as elsewhere, the houses were run-down and vandalized. Shoved roughly from behind, Ben was steered through a jungle-like garden and up the front steps of a dilapidated cottage set well back from the road.

'In there,' Trev said shortly, indicating an open doorway.

The cool pressure of the knife was removed and he stepped hesitantly inside. After the glare of the sunlight he could see very little, only a few uncertain forms hovering in the shadows.

'There you are, Chas,' Trev said confidently, 'told you I'd get him.'

'How d'you know he's the one?' someone asked.

'He's the one all right, no worries.'

As his eyes accustomed themselves to the half-light, he took stock of his surroundings. He was standing in a shabbily furnished room, the windows boarded up, a few strands of sunlight stealing through the cracks between the boards. A number of young men were lounging in old chairs or sitting with their backs against the side walls, watching him. They were all in their early twenties, most of them thin and hollow-eyed, like Trev. There was only one exception: a short, thick-set figure, the sleeves of his denim shirt cut off at the

50

shoulders, revealing powerful arms. Despite the warmth of the afternoon, he was still wearing the woollen balaclava that Ben remembered from the previous night. He came towards Ben now and stood facing him, barely a pace away, his small close-set eyes and the bristly upper portion of his cheeks showing through the balaclava opening.

'You the kid on the bridge last night?' he asked.

'What bridge?'

A hand shot out and slapped him hard across the side of the head.

'Steady on, Chas,' Trev called, and laughed, 'you don't want to damage him. Not a valuable bit of meat like that.'

There was more laughter, only the man called Chas not joining in.

'Let's try again,' he said. 'You the one we chased?'

'Yes.'

'Good. Now just tell me this: how'd you make the dog stand the way it did?'

Ben thought quickly. 'I got him when he was a pup,' he lied, 'years ago, before Last D-. . .'

Again the hand shot out, cutting the word off short. 'We don't talk about that here,' Chas said gruffly.

Ben held his hand to his stinging cheek. 'I had him a long time,' he continued. 'I trained him.'

'You see,' Trev broke in, 'I said we shouldn't have killed it. With him and the dog together, working as a team, we could have pulled it off for sure.'

'We'll manage it anyway,' Chas answered. 'You saw him move: he ran the legs off us. Even on his own he can give us all the time we need.'

'When do we try?' one of the other men asked.

'Tonight.'

'Tonight?' Trev interrupted again. 'But there's a moon! Shouldn't we wait till later?'

Chas brushed past Ben, both fists clenched. 'Didn't I try it in the dark?' he said angrily. 'Before you even got here? The night so black you couldn't see your hand in front of your face. But he saw me all right. Oh yeah, clear as bloody day. That's how I got this!' He pointed at the balaclava covering his head. 'So don't go telling me when's the best time.'

Trev had retreated nervously towards the door. 'Sorry, Chas. Honest. I was only trying to help.'

'You want to help? Then lock the kid up at the back. Give him some food and drink – much as he wants.'

'But . . . '

'And for Chrissake stop arguing! It's only the once, you know that. And we need him in good nick if we're going to have a chance.'

Ben allowed himself to be led over to the door; but just as he was being ushered out, he stopped and turned. 'What do you need me for?' he asked.

The eyes, all that he could see of Chas's face, crinkled up in a knowing smile. 'Oh you needn't worry about that. You'll find out when the time comes. They always do.'

Before he could reply, Trev pushed him roughly through the doorway; and to the general sound of laughter, he walked slowly down the narrow passage.

They let him out of the darkened room at sunset. Just as he was walking back along the passage he again heard that savage cry which always greeted the night, the strong tones reaching out across the silence towards him. Here, so close to the source of that cry, it sounded more defiant, more wild and free, than ever, and he stopped in mid-stride, puzzled by it. Now that he knew where it came from, it simply didn't make sense. Why should any animal still held captive in Taronga Zoo give vent to so passionate a feeling of freedom night after night?

On impulse, he turned towards Trev who was standing impatiently behind him. 'Are you taking me to the Zoo?' he asked. 'Is that what you need me for?'

Trev eyed him suspiciously, his pointed nose thrust forward, his pink-rimmed eyes blinking rapidly in the poor light. 'You been around here before?' he answered.

'No.'

'Then why're you so interested in the Zoo?'

Ben hesitated. 'I . . . I think there's something still in there . . . something big maybe. Any idea what it is?'

Trev's only answer was to grab him by the hair and drag him forcibly into the front room. A single candle was burning in the far corner, the room now empty except for Chas. He turned as they entered, his face still masked by the balaclava.

'We've got a funny one here, Chas,' Trev told him.

'Why, what's up?'

'He already knows something about the Zoo.'

'How much?'

'Hard to say. But we'd better find out before . . .'

His voice trailed away as Chas sauntered across the room and grasped Ben's cheek between thumb and forefinger, twisting the skin until his eyes watered.

'About the Zoo,' he said menacingly, 'you don't happen to come from in there, do you?'

Ben shook his head, his whole face screwed up with pain. There was a pause, the fingers tightening, biting deeper into the flesh.

'And the set-up over there?' Chas added. 'What d'you know about that?'

'Nothing,' Ben answered, his mouth so pulled out of shape that the words came out blurred and indistinct. The fingers relaxed their grip and he went on quickly, 'I heard something this morning, that's all, when I was hiding in the boat. Animal noises.'

Chas released him and looked at Trev. 'That's possible, isn't it?'

'They'd have closed up shop by then,' Trev answered

53

doubtfully. 'The big stuff would've been in anyway.'

'But it's possible?'

'I suppose it's possible. Even so . . .'

Chas waved one hand impatiently. 'Then we'll stick to the plan. I don't reckon he's from in there, that's the main thing, so there's no worry about an ambush. The rest doesn't matter.'

'How'd you make that out?'

'Because once he's inside, he's on his own. What he knows or doesn't know won't help him that much.' He clicked his fingers disdainfully and returned to the far side of the room where he picked up a rifle, left leaning against the wall, and tucked a torch into his belt. 'You ready?' he inquired.

But Trev, still doubtful, lingered by the inner door, a detaining hand on Ben's arm. 'I don't like it,' he murmured sulkily. 'Couldn't we wait a day or two?'

Chas glanced towards him. 'Your trouble, Trev,' he said with a short laugh, 'is that you worry too much. You're like a mouse running round and round a piece of cheese, too scared to eat it.'

'If I'm a mouse,' Trev retaliated unexpectedly, 'what does that make you? Not a cat, that's for sure.'

There was a sudden, tense silence. Ben, who understood little of what was being said, felt the hand gripping his bare arm tighten, the fingers hot with fear.

'Would someone mind letting me . . .' he began, and stopped as he saw the look in Chas's eyes.

'I'd like to make a suggestion,' Chas said at last, his voice fallen to a whisper. 'How about if you take the kid's place?'

The hand on Ben's arm tightened even further. 'No, Chas, not that. I didn't mean anything.'

There was another period of silence, briefer, but no less tense.

'All right, Trev, we'll let it go this time. But I hope for your sake this works tonight. Because if it doesn't, you're next up.

That's a promise.'

He extinguished the candle and led the way out into the heavy dusk, the three of them walking in single file, Ben between the two men. They took the same route Ben had followed that morning, but when they reached the park they turned and made for the strip of thick bush which hugged the shoreline. A lean figure, in the motionless stance of a sentry, was waiting there for them.

'Everyone in position?' Chas asked quietly.

'Yeah, all ready.'

Chas turned to Ben and laid the cool barrel of the rifle across his cheek. 'You stay close to me. And not a sound. Understand?'

'Okay.'

Still in single file, they entered the gloom of the bush. Animal noises, coming from the hillside on their left, disturbed the silence; while on their right, through occasional gaps in the trees, Ben caught glimpses of the wind-ruffled surface of the harbour. The path they were following led them around to the wharf where the ferries carrying passengers to the Zoo had once berthed. The burned-out skeleton of a ferry lay in the shallows and the wharf itself leaned at a crazy angle, some of its wooden piles burned through. But the bitumen road which started opposite the wharf was still in good condition. It ran between the shore and an almost vertical cliff-face and then curved up and around the bush-covered hillside which contained Taronga Zoo. Even in the pale light of the newly risen moon, Ben could see figures stationed along the road. As he watched, two of them padded across the smooth black surface and began scaling the cliff-face, climbing slowly up to the line of bush above.

'Are we going up there?' he asked nervously.

Chas again laid the rifle barrel against his cheek, less gently this time, jarring him backwards. 'No,' he hissed in reply, 'that's just insurance.'

'Insurance?'

The rancid-smelling balaclava moved closer to his face. 'This road here marks the lower edge of the Zoo. Those men are climbing up to the fence. Like everyone else, they'll be making sure you don't take any short cuts.'

Before Ben could ask what that meant, Chas moved off along the road, and he had no option but to hurry after him. In total silence they passed the lower exit – an old square-columned building, the main archway and smaller gates now blocked off – and followed the road for a short distance.

'This is the place,' Chas muttered, 'where the bastard'll be waiting.' And he turned off into the bush on his left.

Ben, hard on his heels, groped his way up a short steep rise and found himself at the base of a low wall. Set into the top of the wall were upright, inward-leaning metal stanchions, with thick strands of barbed wire stretched between them.

'You got those snips?' Chas whispered.

Trev shouldered Ben aside and began cutting through the wire, strand by strand, the blades making a sharp clicking sound as they snapped together. Within a few minutes there was a gap big enough for someone to crawl through.

'Right,' Chas whispered to Ben, 'this is where you do your stuff. When I give the word, you get through that hole and run diagonally across the hillside.' He pointed to a star, low in the sky, to indicate the general direction. 'There'll be cages and things in your way, so fix your eyes on that star or you'll be running round in circles. If you move fast enough, you might make it across the hill to the fence on the far side. Whatever happens, don't try and get out anywhere else. My men'll be on the lookout, and they'll just send you back . . . or worse. Now, have you got all that?'

Ben, crouched close to the wall, looked at the two shapes huddled beside him. 'I don't understand,' he said, bewildered. 'What am I supposed to be doing?'

'Just running.'

'Yes, but what for?'

'Your life.'

'You've told him enough, Chas,' Trev cut in quietly.

But Ben, in a sudden rush of understanding, had already grasped why he had been brought to this spot. As in a dream, he had a vivid impression of a sunlit hillside, with a young dingo peering at him through tall, tufted heads of grass. Yet those amber eyes no longer regarded him with trust. It was as if the gaze of the dead animal were at last demanding vengeance, for itself and all who had shared its fate – with Ben's life now in peril, here on this darker hillside. The roles of hunter and hunted curiously reversed.

'I'm a sort of decoy, aren't I?' he said forlornly.

'That's about it.'

'And if I refuse?'

'I wouldn't advise that.' The rifle was raised, its black silhouette unmistakable against the night sky.

'All right,' Ben answered quietly, 'but at least tell me what I'll be running away from.'

'It wouldn't help you even if you knew.'

'I'd still like you to tell me.'

Chas gave a soft chuckle. 'I'll do better than tell you,' he murmured. He took the torch from his waist and shone the beam on his masked head. Grasping the bottom of the balaclava, he pulled it up, revealing the lower half of his face. It was horribly mutilated, with one ear missing, the mouth torn out of shape, the chin and neck deformed by long raking scars. 'This is what you're running away from, Kid,' he said, and laughed.

Ben flinched back, horrified, as the torch clicked off. 'What could do a thing like that to you?'

By way of answer, there was a deep, full-throated growl from the bush on the far side of the wall. Ben turned, as if to scramble back down the hillside, but strong hands grasped and lifted him towards the gap in the wire. A barbed strand ripped the side of his shirt; and then, despite his frantic resistance, he was through. As he pitched forward into the alien darkness, his arms stretched out to break his fall, a voice half-shouted, 'Run, Kid, run!'

CHAPTER SEVEN

He landed on all fours, the shock of his fall cushioned by the leaf-mould underfoot. Urged on by the voices behind him, he scrambled up the hill, but not very far, aware that he was at his most vulnerable while running blindly. Crouching beneath a cluster of trees that blotted out the pale moonlight, he sent a probing Call into the surrounding gloom. What he detected made him go cold with fright: for close at hand, far closer than he had expected, something was watching him; a creature whose mind was obsessed with a single idea. Hunger. Its own hunger. Everything else excluded. Its eyes, seemingly unhampered by the darkness, fixed upon the pale human figure that crouched in the deep shadows near by.

On the verge of panic, Ben rose to his feet. But even that slight movement produced a rumbling snarl, followed by the sound of a heavy body brushing through the undergrowth. He caught a brief glimpse of a huge tawny head, of amber eyes glinting in the moonlight. And all at once his nerve failed. In blind, thoughtless terror, he turned and began clawing his way through the bush, driving himself up the slope, expecting at every step to feel a massive paw tearing at his head and shoulders. Somewhere, at the back of his mind, the voice of common sense persisted, telling him to stop, to protect himself in the manner he knew best; but he was too frightened to pay it any heed.

Still in a state of panic, he burst out into the open and saw, to his left, a pathway and a flight of steps. Hardly breaking stride, he ran up the steps to a spot where several paths met. There, for the first time, he paused and glanced back: the stairs up which he had come were empty, and when he listened, all he could hear was his own laboured breathing. Again he probed the darkness. To his dismay, he discovered that the creature had circled around him and now lay in wait a short distance ahead. Nor was it alone. Another, similar mind, only slightly less cold and hard, also watched and waited.

Ben's initial instinct was to blot them out, as if by so doing he could reduce them to the level of a bad dream that could be banished by the act of waking. But there was nothing dreamlike about the way the bushes parted, the two creatures stalking out into the open. He could see what they were now. Tigers. One, a lean sinewy female; the other, a huge male, each of his front paws larger than a person's head. They advanced slowly, tails twitching; and Ben, mesmerized by their cool dispassionate gaze, could only stand, transfixed, staring back at them.

The spell was broken by a rumbling snarl, the male's ears suddenly flattening, his snout crinkling up as the beautifully striped cheeks lifted away from the long pale canines.

'No!' Ben shouted, his hands jerking up before him in a futile gesture of defence, his mind automatically sending out a frantic danger warning.

It was that wordless signal which stopped them, both animals balking only a few paces from where Ben stood. He repeated the same warning, and this time the female backed off slightly. But not the male. Swinging his head from side to side, he roared his bewilderment out into the night, his rank breath like a gust of hot wind on Ben's face.

'Go!' Ben Called, trying to order them away, but the silent

60

command was too lacking in conviction to be effective. Faced with so much savage power, all he could think of was escape, of somehow reaching the low wall and the gap in the barbed wire. He had forgotten Chas's threat about what might happen if he turned back. At that moment the wall and the human beings on the other side conveyed to him only the idea of safety. All that kept him rooted to this one spot was the sure knowledge that if he turned and ran, those vast paws would destroy him.

So he stood there, unmoving, caught up in a strange, unnerving form of stalemate, with the male tiger continuing to roar at him. Had that situation gone on much longer, there could have been only one result – Ben's resolve already wilting beneath that defiant gaze. But from the darkness up ahead there came a sound of rapid footsteps, someone small and light running towards him.

'Over here!' he called desperately, making the mistake of taking his eyes from the menacing head.

It was only a momentary lapse of concentration, yet enough for the tiger to glide forward and strike at him, the huge paw just missing his face, the wind of its passage fanning his cheek so that he fell back, both arms curled protectively about his head. Out of the corner of his eye, he saw a shadowy figure which, in his fear, he mistook for the female tiger, also closing in on him.

'No!' he signalled desperately, 'no!'

And almost simultaneously, someone said aloud, 'Back Raja, back. Ranee, back' – the words soothing and gentle, more of an appeal than a command.

Afterwards, he had no doubt that it was that softly spoken appeal which saved him, though at the time he felt only a flood of relief at finding himself still alive. He looked up and saw that the tigers had sidled away; saw also that a young Aboriginal girl was standing close to him. She was about his own age, but much smaller, at least a head shorter than himself, with thin, stick-like arms and legs, and skin and hair so black that they almost merged into the background darkness.

'Where are the others?' she asked, all the gentleness gone from her voice now.

'Others?'

'Your mates, where are they?'

'I'm on my own. I only . . . '

She clicked her tongue and the male tiger, pacing restlessly to and fro, rumbled out a threatening growl.

'Hang on!' he protested. 'They sent me in and told me to run. I don't know any more than that!'

She crouched beside him and looked searchingly into his face – her own face, he noticed, distinctly young and smooth, marred only by a line of worry that creased her forehead. 'You sure?' she asked. 'Because if you're lying . . . '

'I'm not lying. I swear! They didn't even tell me about the tigers. I just heard this growl and then they pushed me through the gap in the wire.'

'So they're not your mates?'

He shook his head.

'But they are out there now?'

'Yes, down by the wall.' He turned and pointed in the direction of the harbour. 'And more of them along the lower fence.'

She stood up slowly, obviously undecided, her even white teeth biting at her lip. The male tiger, meanwhile, had again ceased his restless pacing and was glowering at Ben dangerously.

'Listen,' he said intently, 'you've got to believe me! They made me help them. I didn't want to. Not after . . . after the way they killed . . . ' But even then, in that situation, he could not bring himself to say it.

She nodded, responding more to the emotion in his voice than to the actual words. 'Okay,' she said, more kindly. 'Wait here for a while. I won't be long. Whatever happens don't move or make a noise, because there's more than these tigers on the loose.'

She gave him no chance to argue. With a soft click of her tongue she ran off down the steps, the two tigers loping after her. Left alone, Ben crawled into the cover of the nearest bushes and waited, his eyes nervously searching the shadows, his ears alert to the faintest noise. But nothing else ventured near and she was soon back, alone this time, running effortlessly up the steps.

'Quick!' she said urgently. 'We have to get well clear. Once they start I won't be able to control them.'

'Start what?'

'I can't explain. Just hurry!'

Ben leaped to his feet, thinking he would easily catch up with her, but even at his fastest he could barely match her pace, her thin legs carrying her rapidly along the maze of winding paths. Although he had often visited the Zoo with his parents, years before, he soon had only the vaguest idea of where they were, the route they were taking leading steadily uphill, past the gaunt outline of wire cages and dark, closed-up buildings.

'Where're we heading?' he called breathlessly.

Her reply was cut short by an agonized scream which came from directly behind him, though some distance down the hill.

'What was that?' he asked, stopping in the middle of the pathway.

She looked back, her expression veiled by the shadows that fell across her face. 'I told you, once they start there's no stopping them. We could be next if we're not careful.'

'Us?'

Another terrible scream, closer and slightly to his left, rang out.

'Yes, us,' she said, her voice low, almost expressionless. 'It's

63

the smell. They go for anyone after they've scented it.'

'You mean . . . blood?'

She made no reply, standing there looking at him.

'Are you telling me those tigers are killing the men down there?' he burst out.

'Not just the tigers.'

'But that's why you led them off?' he insisted.

'I thought those blokes weren't your friends!' she flared back.

'To go and kill them like that!'

She walked hurriedly towards him, her face, streaked with moonlight, looking sad and tired. 'If it wasn't for the animals,' she said, her voice tightly controlled, 'what do you reckon the men would do to us? Haven't you worked out why they put you through the wire?'

He knew what she said made sense, but the whole situation was too much like – again he shied away from the memory: the dog's dying scream still too vivid.

'But they're human beings,' he objected, 'not animals' – realizing as he spoke that he was no longer accusing her: merely justifying himself. 'And their bodies! If we leave them down there . . . '

'It was their choice,' she said regretfully, making no attempt now to hide her true feelings. 'They understood what they were coming into. There's nothing we can do to help them.'

'Nothing?'

'I'm afraid not,' she said, slipping her hand through his arm. 'Now come on. Please. It's not safe here.'

She pulled gently and he allowed himself to be led away, the two of them continuing along the paths.

Once more, before they could find a place of safety, a dying scream disturbed the night, but this time he didn't slow down, running with his hands over his ears, his shoulders hunched forward defensively.

64

When they finally stopped he recognized the place immediately. A large rambling building – made mainly of wood and
with a red-tiled roof – it had once been the restaurant and
shop as well as housing the information offices. Now it was
sunk in darkness, the long front windows shuttered from
within. The girl approached the front door and tapped lightly.
There were furtive footsteps inside and a man's voice asked,
'Who's there?'

'It's me, Ellie.'

The door opened a crack and she slipped through, drawing
Ben after her.

'What the hell!'

The shout of surprise came from a young man at the door.
He was tall and lean-featured, with jet-black hair. Before Ellie
could try to explain, he pounced on Ben and pinned both
arms behind him.

'What's this then?' he asked accusingly, driving his knee
painfully into Ben's back.

'No, leave him, Steve!' Ellie said quickly. 'He's not with the
others. He was just bait, to keep Raja off.'

'Says who?'

'Me. I've been down there.'

'So why'd you bring him back? If he's bait, then let the cats
have him.'

He made as if to re-open the door, but Ellie barred his way.
'He hasn't done anything, Steve! Really.'

'Clear out or you'll join him.'

'At least tell Molly. Let her decide.'

He took one hand off Ben and lunged at her, his bare
knuckles crashing against the wooden panelling as she
slipped beneath his arm.

'What's going on over there?' a woman's voice called
indignantly.

'I'll fix you one of these days, Ellie,' Steve muttered.

But he made no further attempt to throw Ben out. Still

65

holding him firmly, he pushed him past a flight of wooden stairs and across a wide, shadowy room towards the serving bay of the restaurant. A large, slightly overweight woman was sitting on the counter. She was in her mid-thirties, with blonde hair and a hard attractive face. There was a telephone and a kerosene pressure lamp beside her.

'Where'd that come from?' she said shortly, speaking of Ben as if he were some lifeless object.

'Ellie brought him back,' Steve answered. 'Says they were using him as bait.'

She turned her hard green eyes towards the young Aboriginal girl. 'D'you think you're indispensable or something?' she asked softly.

Ellie grew suddenly nervous, both bare feet shuffling on the smooth floor. 'No, Molly, I was only . . . '

'Because if you do, I'll be glad to prove how wrong you are.'

'I'm sorry, Molly' - eyes downcast, her feet still now.

'Right. So just remember in future, this isn't a welfare society. We don't take in the leftovers that rabble out there push over the fence.'

'That's what I told her,' Steve said. 'Shall I chuck him out?'

Her eyes narrowed thoughtfully. 'No, not yet.' She looked directly at Ben for the first time. 'You, what's your name?'

He tried to stare back defiantly, but there was an unyielding quality about her face that daunted him and, like Ellie, he also dropped his gaze.

'Ben,' he said uneasily.

'Tell me, Ben, how many of them are trying to break in?'

'I'm not sure. Quite a lot I think.'

She nodded. 'That's my feeling too.' She patted the telephone beside her and turned back to Steve. 'By the sound of things, the cats've probably got more than enough to do at the moment. Perhaps it'd be better for him to stick around here for a while.'

'Yeah, that's not a bad idea,' Steve conceded. 'Shall I put him upstairs?'

'No, leave him here where I can keep an eye on him.'

Steve gave his arm a final wrench and then shoved him away so violently that he crashed against the counter and slid onto the floor. But for the moment he didn't care – the tight knot of anxiety, which had been there in the pit of his stomach ever since Chas had forced him through the wire, at last beginning to ease.

'You mean he can stay?' Ellie asked hopefully.

Molly stretched lazily. 'You were the one who referred to him as bait, Ellie, isn't that right?'

'Yes.'

'Well, haven't you ever been fishing?'

'With my dad, before . . . ' She corrected herself quickly. 'A long time ago.'

'And what did you do with your spare bait at the end of the day?'

Ellie didn't answer, her bare feet again beginning their nervous shuffling.

'Don't you remember?'

Still she remained silent, and Ben, watching her, felt the knot of anxiety reforming in his stomach.

'Then I'll jog your memory,' Molly said with mock pleasantness. 'You throw it in the water. It's no good to you any more, so you give the fish a free feed.'

CHAPTER EIGHT

Slumped in the corner, Ben looked unhappily at the room in which, three years earlier, he had sat with his parents. The windows had been open then, the overhead fans turning slowly, making the big paper lampshades swing lazily in the breeze, and children had been running in and out, laughing and calling to each other, dodging between the tables and chairs and the square wooden columns that supported the broad span of roof and ceiling. Physically, it had not changed very much: the tables and chairs were still there, though stacked in the far corner; and the lampshades and fans, useless in the absence of power, still hung from the ceiling. The real change, he realized, was in the atmosphere of the room. The sense of space and freedom were gone, replaced by something else. Not just a feeling of tension – that was understandable on a night like this. It was more as if this whole building had become a part of the caged world of the Zoo, a general feeling of sadness infecting the air. The hopelessness of Last Days persisting here as well, despite everyone's refusal to acknowledge or mention it.

Ben leaned his head back against the wall and closed his eyes, trying to conserve his energies for what might lie ahead. But he found it impossible to rest. The night continued to be disturbed by painful cries, and once even by a gunshot – a distant explosion that brought three young people clattering down the stairs, rifles in hand, ready to reinforce the guard at the door. Less than a minute later the phone jangled, an uneven ring of the kind made by someone winding a manual machine. Molly picked up the receiver, and from the way she spoke Ben gathered that the telephone service was part of an internal system, working only within the confines of the Zoo.

'It's all right,' she called out, replacing the receiver, 'it was one of ours. They picked off a straggler trying to break into the house.'

Not long after that there was hammering on the front door, accompanied by an hysterical voice pleading for help. Steve again came round to the counter.

'Should we put him out of his misery?' he asked casually.

Molly shook her head. 'Better leave him,' she advised coolly, 'just in case it's a trick.'

Yet even Ben could tell that there was nothing false about those sobbing cries. For the second time that night he covered his ears, but the cries were too loud to be so easily blocked out, gradually working up to a crescendo, a long mournful scream that ceased abruptly. Hesitantly, he took his hands from his ears and listened: all he could hear now was a snuffling animal noise, coming from just outside the door, followed by the faint scraping sound of a body being dragged away.

'You murdered him!' he muttered, wanting to scream at Molly, to make her understand what she had done. But when he turned towards her, she was half asleep, the incident already forgotten; and like Ellie much earlier, he said nothing, too overcome by his own feelings of helplessness.

That proved to be the final disturbance of the night. An uneasy silence settled upon Taronga, the hours dragging by, with Molly occasionally jerking awake to call out to Steve at the main door or to ring through to one of the other strongholds within the grounds. For the first few hours Ben sat straight and still in the corner, convinced that he could never sleep in such a place, his whole body hot and sticky, as though drenched in the blood that had been spilled. But as the night wore on, tired out by tension and fear, he also began to doze.

He was woken by loud voices. He had no idea what time it was, whether dawn had broken or not, because the windows remained shuttered, the room still lit by pressure lamps. Groggy with sleep, he sat up and saw that Ellie was standing only a few paces away, arguing with Molly and Steve, her thin dark body stiff and defiant.

'But you can't!' she was saying. 'It's not fair!'

'Fair?' Molly said scornfully. 'Nothing's fair any more, girl. Or hadn't you noticed?'

'But he hasn't done anything!'

'He let himself get caught. Isn't that enough?'

'It's no reason to treat him like ... like ... '

'Like meat?' Steve cut in quickly. 'Why not? The cats have to eat too.'

Ellie rounded on him angrily. 'You're worse than Raja, d'you know that? He at least kills for food. But you ... !'

Without warning, Steve lashed out and caught her a vicious blow on the neck, knocking her to the floor. As she struggled to rise, he closed in, clenched fist raised.

'No, leave her!' Ben called, lurching to his feet.

Steve whirled around. His face, distorted by anger, suddenly reminded Ben of Greg – the same lean hard features devoid of any depth of feeling; the same mindless fury bursting out of him.

'There's no point in fighting over me,' he said evenly. 'I'm going anyway.'

'Too right you are!'

'I mean now. I'm ready.'

'You don't have to play the hero with us,' Molly said drily.

'I'm not a hero,' he answered, and meant it. Because the prospect of going outside alone was not particularly frightening. He knew that this time, if he didn't panic, he had a good chance of making it to the outer fence. The thing that really bothered him was the thought of what lay beyond the fence: the equally savage world of the city; the crumbling, hopeless streets.

'C'mon,' he said, 'let's get it over with.'

He had wanted to sound relaxed, unflurried, but his voice betrayed him, coming out in a strangled whisper. Steve, his anger rapidly subsiding, grinned broadly at him, his lean cheeks creasing around the mouth.

'Like a lamb to the slaughter,' he said, and then added lightly, 'Don't worry, it'll soon be over. They're real quick, those pets of ours.'

Ben shrugged and walked slowly towards the door.

'You can't let him go out there!' Ellie cried. 'Not tonight! You know what'll happen!'

He paused and glanced back. She was looking not at him, but at Molly, the smooth black skin of her forehead again marred by a deep furrow of concern.

'Let him stay,' she pleaded. 'Please, Molly. He can help me with the caging. You said yourself that we need someone else.'

'What's so special about him?' Molly asked.

'Raja trusts him.'

'No, Ellie, you're the only one Raja trusts.'

'But when I found him, down near the concert stage, Raja and Ranee hadn't hurt him.'

'Perhaps they got to him the same time as you.'

'No, Raja had already charged. I saw him strike and miss. And he never misses unless he means to.'

Molly turned to Steve. 'What d'you think?'

'She'd say anything to save him. You know what she's like.'

'But what if it's true?'

'There's one way to find out.'

Molly drew both hands down her face in a tired, impatient

71

gesture. 'Steve's right,' she said to Ellie. 'If he wants to stay, he has to prove he's some use.'

'He will,' Ellie answered eagerly. 'I'll take him out with me later and . . . '

'No, not with you. Alone.'

'Alone?' Her face registered sudden alarm. 'That's asking too much, especially tonight.'

'It's tonight or never.'

'But . . . '

Molly waved one hand irritably. 'No more arguments, Ellie. Everyone here has to earn their keep. He can start earning his tonight, by getting the tigers in. That'll do for starters. Now let him get on with it. Steve'll show him the layout.'

She turned her back abruptly, as though dismissing the whole matter from her mind, and walked over to the phone where she began ringing through to the other strongholds, making a final check that all was quiet.

'What exactly are you expecting me to do?' Ben asked apprehensively.

Still grinning, obviously enjoying the situation, Steve picked up a lamp and led him to where a large map of the Zoo had been pinned to the wall.

'Here's where you are now,' he said, stabbing a sinewy finger at a point more than two-thirds of the way up the hillside. 'And down here, below us, are the tiger cages. The wooden doors leading to the back of the cages will be open. All you have to do is get the tigers through that door and into the cage at the far end.' He chuckled at the prospect. 'You have half an hour – no more – because the other animals still have to be caged before dawn. For their safety, as well as yours.' Again he chuckled. 'You got all that?'

Ben studied the network of paths in that quarter of the Zoo. 'I've got it,' he said shortly.

But at the door Ellie gripped his arm tightly and held him

72

back. With the light behind her, she looked very small and frail, her great bush of black hair seemingly too heavy for her meagre body.

'When you find them,' she said, speaking so quickly that the words almost ran together, 'it's Raja you have to watch. If you can control him, Ranee'll follow. But don't take your eyes off either of them, not for a second. And talk to them all the time. You know, real soft and friendly, the way you'd talk to people.'

' . . . to people,' he repeated uneasily.

'Come on,' Steve said, unbolting the door and opening it a crack, allowing the cool night air to seep in.

'Just one more thing,' Ellie added urgently, still clutching at his arm. 'To get them in the cage, you'll need some . . . some meat. They won't go in without it.' She turned her head slightly, her features catching the light, and he saw an agonized expression flit across her face. 'So . . . so try and collect some.'

'Meat?' he asked.

'Yes, if you can' – her voice small, refusing to remain steady.

'But there's only . . . ' He too hesitated, grasping her meaning, his body shuddering involuntarily at the idea.

'It's the only kind the tigers'll take tonight,' she said quickly.

'No!' He closed the discussion with an abrupt movement of his hand. 'I couldn't do that.'

'You have to!' Her shoulders quivering as she struggled silently with herself as well as with him. 'I know it sounds . . . but it's your only chance.'

'I'm sorry, I just couldn't.'

Prising her fingers from his arm, he stepped quickly through the opening, hearing the faint click of the door closing behind him.

Outside, it was quiet and very nearly still, only a murmur of breeze drifting across the hillside, bringing with it the faintly metallic smell of the sea. He remained in the doorway a minute or two, allowing his eyes to grow accustomed to the moonlight, but also giving himself time to reach a decision. One of the things the map had shown him was that the restaurant was very close to the side boundary of the Zoo. If he were to send out a danger warning, the area would probably remain clear long enough for him to reach the fence. But what then? Where would he go next? To Coogee? No, that had been a dream, a part of his life which, sadly, could never be recaptured. His recent experiences of the city had convinced him of that.

But if not his former home, then where? There was only one other alternative: to stay here; to go down into the darkness and face the tigers. The idea appalled him. As, in a different way, did the prospect of joining forces with Molly and Steve – both of them too much like Greg, people who had paid too high a price for survival. Yet at least Ellie was here. Ellie, the one bright spot of sanity in all this madness; human warmth and pity still alive in her. He touched his arm, where her fingers had gripped his flesh so protectively, all his instincts telling him that if he ran from her as he had from everything else, he would also be sucked into the general madness eventually. And anything was preferable to that.

With what resolution he could muster, he stepped out into the waning moonlight and looked around. Not far from where he stood, there was an open-sided rotunda which had once offered shade to visitors to the Zoo. Now something else stirred within it: predatory eyes peering at him; a large feline body, smaller than a tiger but still powerful about the shoulders, crouched above its prey; a bloodied mouth nuzzling at the grisly remains of torn limbs. Remembering those frantic cries, the fists pounding at the door, Ben had to fight down an almost overwhelming feeling of repugnance. Clearing his mind, he forced himself to send out a gentle, welcoming Call. He was prepared for a savage outburst; but what he received instead, after a brief hesitation, was an eager response of the kind he might have expected from the dog had it still been alive; the soundless reply reinforced by a purring growl that drew him into an invisible circle of warmth and trust.

He edged away, guiltily, gazing into the night, allowing his mind to open fully, to reach out over the hillside. Straight away the Zoo, previously so dark and still, burst into life all about him, hundreds of minds awakening to his Call. Oddly elated, he began running along the path, working his way steadily downhill, searching. Other sinister forms responded from the shadows – a lion, a pair of cheetahs – their soft growls caressing him as he hurried past. But not only predators responded to the Call: he soon discovered that there were scores of non-predatory animals in the Zoo, antelope and deer, goats, camels, giraffes, and many more, all of them somehow secure, unworried by the darkness and the prowling cats. That puzzled him for a while, until he paused beside what had originally been a large aviary and heard the contented sounds of munching from within. Then, for the first time, he began to understand what Taronga had become, and also why people like Chas wanted to take it over.

Yet such discoveries did not occupy him for long. His main concern, all the time, was the tigers, and he found them at last down near the lower fence, close to where Ellie had left them.

Ranee was the one he located first. Suspicious to begin with, she half-closed her mind against him before responding in a warm rush of trust – the same simple trust that had ensured his survival over the past two years. Guessing that her mate would be near by, he Called again, and detected a wall of silence. He probed deeper, piercing the wall, releasing an outburst of defiance that brought him stumbling to a halt.

'Come,' he Called enticingly, trying to break down the animal's resistance, using all his talent to search out an area of

75

weakness. But there was none, the tiger's mind as firm, as immovable, as the ground beneath Ben's feet, with distrust rooted there like some deadly flower bursting from the soil. And something else lurking there as well, which Ben could not quite identify.

With halting steps, he crept through the heavy bush. He knew the tigers were close, dangerously so, the sounds of their feeding, the scraping of teeth upon bone, reaching him clearly. Easing aside a leafy branch, he peered down into a small open space, sensing that they were here, in front of him, yet unable to separate their striped bodies from the streaks of moonlight and shadow that patterned the ground.

'Ranee,' he whispered aloud.

She moved, the whole scene springing into focus, and he found himself staring at the mangled remnants of a body, the human limbs barely identifiable. Ben gagged at the sight, holding his hand over his mouth to contain his rising gorge. He thought for a moment that he was going to faint, and it was only the fear of what would follow which enabled him to bring his churning stomach under control.

He could see them both now: two powerful animals crouching side by side, their bodies blending into the shadows, their chests and muzzles, the insides of their front legs, stained an ominous black. They were watching him, and when he gestured silently, Ranee rose, ready to follow him up the slope. It was only Raja who prevented her: shouldering her aside, he stood menacingly in the centre of the clearing, a deep growl rumbling in his throat.

'It's all right,' Ben murmured softly. 'We're friends now, friends.'

But there was no friendship in that watchful stare, and when Ben reached through the darkness and the silence and brushed the animal's mind with his own, he felt as if he were making contact with a searing flame, his whole body starting back in alarm. Yet Raja remained unmoved, holding the same

76

aggressive stance. And all at once Ben realized what it was he had detected earlier when he had forced his way through Raja's protective wall of silence. Hatred. That and nothing else. The proud, savage mind of the creature perceiving in him a symbol of the whole hated human species. His youthful image filling those glowing eyes. And not without reason: for whereas people like Molly and Steve had merely restricted the tiger's physical freedom, he, Ben, was trying to lure his mind into submission; to betray him even further; to reduce him to the level of a tame dog . . . Yes, simply that, a tame dog.

The sheer intensity of the tiger's dislike made Ben clutch both hands to his head, though strangely he felt no resentment. He even understood the animal's hatred of him. 'Yes, I know,' he said aloud, 'I know' – hearing again the countless rifle shots that had rung out across countless hillsides; feeling that other rifle within his hands, the barrel probing for the hollow of the horse's temple; recapturing those first moments with the dog, the way it had whimpered and come to him, crawling forward on its belly.

'I know,' he repeated, wanting to convey to the tiger all his accumulated regret. But it was impossible. The gulf between them was too great. And when he again groped clumsily for the mind of the other, all he encountered was a growing tension as the animal gathered himself into a tight knot of explosive energy. Ben saw then what he should have been aware of all along: the heavy shoulder muscles drawing together; the tip of the tail twitching erratically; the broad front paws gently kneading the earth as they sought for a firm grip.

He had no need to think, his own survival instinct taking over completely. Abandoning all attempt at friendly communication, he sent out a single command, issuing it with all the power he could manage. The effect was instantaneous. Raja reared back, snarling, spitting at him, front paws swiping at the air in an effort to break free. Ben held on grimly, their two

77

minds locked in a battle of wills, each in his own way fighting for his life.

With the same caution he had used in approaching the clearing, Ben backed slowly up the hill, drawing the two animals after him. Ranee remained docile, her lithe body cowering submissively; only Raja continued to roar out a protest, his ears flattened to his skull, his hindquarters hugging the ground. Yet step by step he too followed Ben, unable to sever the invisible bond that linked him to this hated figure.

When they reached the path, Ben relaxed his grip, allowing Raja to circle about him. He sensed, rightly, that the male would not wander far from his mate, and so he held her there on the path with him, using her as a kind of bait, much as he had been used earlier, exerting only enough mental force to protect himself from sudden attack. Even so, the slow journey up the hillside required an effort of will that sapped his energy, and by the time they reached the tiger cages his ragged clothes were sticking to his body.

'Inside, Ranee,' he whispered, thinking that once again Raja would follow.

He stepped aside as she slunk through the open doorway; but this time Raja refused to approach, roaring at him from the shadows. Closing his eyes, he concentrated on forcing the animal to obey. Yet still, although he brought the tiger to within metres of the doors, he couldn't make him enter the building.

'Meat,' Ellie had whispered hesitantly, 'they won't go in without it.' But he could not revert to that, no matter what the consequences. Which left only one course of action. The hardest part of all: to enter the dark tunnel himself.

Stepping inside was like stepping into nothing. Total blackness. A lightless world defined by smell rather than sight or touch – the rank scent of feline bodies permeating the air. Somewhere, nearby, he could sense Ranee's crouching presence, her eyes attuned to such darkness. Here, in this confined space, he could not rely on controlling both animals – it was asking too much – and reluctantly he released her, proffering her the same wordless trust that she had given him so freely.

Able now to focus all his attention on Raja, he turned towards the open doorway – only to find that Raja was already there, framed by the square opening. Quickly Ben stopped his forward momentum, renewing the struggle. It was the kind of combat which, ultimately, he could never hope to win, but for the present it was all that stood between him and those cunningly sheathed claws. Slowly he backed away along the dark tunnel, forcing Raja to follow, never taking his eyes from that shape outlined against the receding doorway, never allowing his attention to wander except for once, by accident.

He was very near the end of the tunnel, and as Ranee sidled invisibly past him, gliding towards the door of the cage, the coarse fur of her cheek and neck brushed against his bare leg. Startled, he leaped aside, his concentration wavering. There was a sound of soft pads striking the concrete floor, the distant doorway vanishing, swallowed by the blackness and Raja was there, looming over him, his coughing grunt filling the gloomy tunnel and echoing amongst the empty cages. How close Ben came to death he never knew, because of the darkness; but when, Calling frantically, he managed to halt the charge, Raja was barely an arm's length from him, one paw already raised and ready to strike.

'Back, Raja, back,' he whispered, using the same words, the same tone of voice, that Ellie had used in similar circumstances.

But not with the same effect, for the animal stayed where he was, his rasping breath wafting past Ben's face. So that finally it was Ben himself who backed away, with Raja stalking forward, the boy and the tiger moving in unison, as if connected by some unseen leash or tie.

A nerve-racking few minutes followed, with the two adversaries matching each other's movements perfectly – the tension only relieved when Ben, reaching behind him, located the open doorway of the last cage in the row. Hastily, he stepped beyond the opening.

'Inside!' he commanded, willing the animal to do his bidding, drawing on all his remaining strength.

For a time Raja resisted, the outline of his head unmoving, as though fixed in space, a terrifying shape placed there to test Ben's waning courage. He hung on grimly, his own accelerating heartbeat pounding in his ears, and not until it seemed that he must give in, what was left of his strength and courage drawn out like a brittle thread that might break at any second, did that fearful head move, dipping forward and down. Letting out a last fierce roar of defiance that shook the whole building, Raja vanished from sight, padding soundlessly off into the obscure depths of the cage.

With a loud clang, Ben slid the raised door down into place. Something rattled close to his hand, a padlock hanging loosely from the bars, and he tore it clear and hooked it through the locking hasp, clicking it closed and pulling out the key.

At last he allowed his control to lapse. Severely shaken, he slumped to his knees, eyes closed, and leaned his forehead against the cool vertical metal bars. And that was when Raja, still alert, still undefeated, made his most determined challenge of the night. Leaping swiftly across the cage, he struck at the kneeling figure, aiming at the head. Had the bars been further apart, the contest between them might have ended there. As it was, Raja's paw merely slammed into the unyielding steel, sending Ben reeling backwards, his head ringing from the violence of the blow.

He was up again immediately. Physically, he was unharmed, but the shock of that unexpected assault, added to the constant strain of the past half hour, was too much for him. And with a feeble cry he ran from the building and up along the winding paths.

Minutes later he was pounding on the restaurant door, begging to be allowed in, his pleading cries echoing those of the unknown man earlier in the night. The door opened and he staggered inside, Steve catching him by the scruff of the neck and preventing him from falling. Something slipped from his hand and slithered across the floor.

'I'm sorry, Greg,' he sobbed, 'honest, Greg, I'm sorry' – not knowing for the moment where he was; aware only that in some obscure way he had failed.

Molly, until then dozing by the telephone, hurried from the far side of the room. 'What's happened?' she asked suspiciously.

Other figures were already pounding down the stairs.

'Looks to me as though Raja chased him back here,' Steve answered with a sneer.

But Ellie, who had been searching the floor area close to the door, suddenly stood up, her eyes round with astonishment. 'No!' she said, bursting into laughter and holding the key up for them all to see. 'He did it! He caged the tigers!'

CHAPTER NINE

He awoke feeling rested and refreshed. Although the sun was still high, there in the deep shade of a tall Moreton Bay fig tree it was pleasantly cool, the breeze from the harbour gently stirring the leaves above his head. He sat up and stretched, the sudden movement startling a herd of small antelope that edged nervously away across the grassy slope. Other animals grazed or browsed near by. The long-lipped, slightly comical head of a giraffe peered at him from the other side of a dense clump of bamboo; guinea fowl and geese mingled in the speckled shade of a jacaranda, picking their way through the purple carpet of fallen blossoms; further up the slope, deer and barbary sheep fed quietly on grass and bushes that flourished beneath a line of palms. Beyond the palms, just visible amidst so much abundant growth, there was a long row of cages, empty now, their doors standing open.

'How does it look in daylight?' someone asked.

He turned and saw Ellie walking jauntily across the grass towards him, her mop of unruly hair a glossy black in the sun.

'Like the Garden of Eden,' he said, and laughed.

She pulled a wry face. 'I hope paradise was better than this.'

'You must admit, though,' he insisted, 'the animals do live in a sort of harmony.'

She grew suddenly serious. 'Not with people they don't. You heard those screams last night the same as I did.'

The smile vanished from his face. 'Let's forget about that,' he mumbled.

'You can't. Not in here. You're always being reminded.'

'Is it often like that?'

'It wasn't at first. While there were still houses to be looted, we had hardly any trouble from outside. But since the food supply ran out things've got steadily worse.'

'So last night wasn't unusual?'

'Not really. It's what you can expect if you stay. Like I said, this isn't really paradise: it's more like what was left after they messed it up. You know, ate the apple and all that stuff – found out things.'

He glanced sideways at her, almost furtively. 'What did they find out? In Eden, I mean.'

She shrugged her thin shoulders. 'I reckon I can guess. Can't you?'

But he didn't answer, staring gloomily at a small mob of cattle and antelope being driven along the path below him by a young man and woman.

'Talking of finding out things,' Ellie said lightly, trying to strike a more cheerful note, 'have you found out how this place works?'

'It's a kind of farm, isn't it? With the harmless animals taken out to feed during the day, but then locked up at night for safekeeping.'

She nodded. 'That's more or less it. Though it's a fortress too. Especially after dark, when we free the cats. Without them, none of this would have lasted five minutes.'

'That's something I don't really understand,' he admitted. 'Why do the attacks always come at night? Wouldn't it be easier to try and get in during the day?'

'No, it'd be harder still. Except for us, everyone here is armed.' She pointed to the two people herding animals along the lower path. 'See those rifles they're carrying: they're the best you can get, pinched from a military camp. You'd stand less chance against them than against Raja.'

The young man, seeing her pointing at him, waved back. He was strongly built, with small close-set eyes and a thin expressionless mouth. 'Lazing around as usual,' he called out.

'You jealous?' she replied. 'Like to change jobs?'

'Not a chance. I'd rather look after these' – indicating the animals on the path – 'than any of those cats.'

'That's Terry,' Ellie confided to Ben, 'and the girl with him is Val. They look friendly enough now, but they're both pretty hard cases.'

'How'd they get here?'

'The same as everyone else: Molly chose them. She only picks the really tough ones. People who think the way she does. That's why this place is still intact.'

'And Molly? When did she arrive?'

'She might have been here all along. It's hard to say. You know what people are like, they won't talk about Last Days.'

'You don't seem to mind mentioning it,' he said.

She gave him a sudden proud look. 'Why should I? I'm Aboriginal. We don't forget about things that easy. We have our stories to remind us. My dad always reckoned that's why we've survived as a people. Because we remember so much, even the bad things.'

Ben frowned, aware of his own repeated attempts to forget the events of the past. 'I'm not sure I follow all that,' he said uneasily.

'It's simple,' she answered brightly. 'My dad explained it to me. He said being alive is like going on a journey: you never really know where you are unless you remember how you got there.'

'And how did we get here?' he asked bitterly.

'Oh, dad told me about that too. He . . . '

But he cut her short impatiently. 'Why d'you have to talk

about your father all the time? He's dead. Leave him in peace.'

'But he's my father,' she said disarmingly. 'He didn't just vanish into thin air. When I think about him, it's like he was still here.'

'That's a load of garbage!' Ben said, hearing the harshness in his own voice, but unable to prevent it. 'You're just kidding yourself. Your dad and all the rest of them are gone. They might as well never have existed!'

Ellie leaped to her feet, more astonished than angry. 'I thought you were different from this,' she said. 'But you're like all the others. Like Molly and Steve. That's the way they talk, as if they never knew anybody before they came here.'

Shamefaced, he reached up and took her hand, drawing her down beside him once again. 'I'm sorry,' he murmured. 'I didn't mean to sound like them. It's just that it's hard even to think about some things.'

'But that's why you *have* to think about them,' she said reasonably. 'Otherwise you end up the same as Molly and Steve. People with nothing left inside them. Steve especially.'

'You don't like him, do you?'

'No, but I try not to show it. After Molly, he's the most important person around.'

Involuntarily, he pictured Steve's lean-featured face, his likeness to Greg. It occurred to him that Trev, if he weren't so thin and undernourished, would have the same kind of look.

'What's so important about him?' he asked. 'I've seen plenty of people like that.'

'You may have. But Molly needs Steve – that's the difference – because of what he can do. He's pretty clever when it comes to practical things. After the water supply packed up, he was the one who found the original spring and fed it back into the upper ponds. He did lots of other things too. He rigged up a sort of windmill for charging a whole lot of batteries. Then he fixed the telephones and attached an alarm system to the outer fence.'

'How'd he rig the alarm system?' Ben asked.

'I'm not too sure, because I don't know much about electrical things. But there're thin wires running round the inside of the fence, fixed to it, but sort of insulated from it as well. You can't get through without touching one of those thin wires and that sets off buzzers in all the main buildings. Sometimes they're set off by the animals brushing against a wire, but not often. Usually it's more serious than that. Like last night.'

He nodded, trying not to betray his feelings. But the talk of Steve and the reference to the previous night seemed to cast a pall over the day. The park lay before him exactly as before: green and lush, with the cages thrown open and the animals roaming freely where once only people had walked. Except that now it was as if a thin film of cloud had passed across the sun, tingeing everything with grey. He turned towards Ellie and saw for the first time how completely out of place she was there: her face open and unspoiled, her thin body quick and full of life.

'You didn't say how you managed to end up in Taronga,' he said.

'Oh, the same as you,' she answered, and laughed as though it were a joke. 'I was pushed through the fence one night, as bait. I didn't have a clue where I was or what I was supposed to do. That's why I believed you last night. I know what it's like landing here in the dark and hearing something growl in the bushes.'

The terrifying reality of that moment came rushing back to him. 'What did you do?' he asked tensely.

Yet that same memory, apparently, held no terrors for Ellie. She laughed again. 'Nothing much. I made lots of soothing noises and crawled around in the dark mostly. In the end, I somehow found my way up to the restaurant. It was just luck really, but Molly's pretty sharp. She saw straight away that I might be useful. The next night she had me getting the cats in.'

'Weren't you scared?'

'I was at first. It wasn't too bad, though. Before I came, nets and guns were used to round up the cats. That must have been tough, because the cats got used to guns a long time ago – they had to, to survive. For them, the sound of a rifle means meat, and once they hear a shot they're real difficult to manage. With me working on my own it was different. Everything was quiet and they weren't excited or anything. All I had to do was coax them a bit. Raja was the only tricky one. He never wants to give up his freedom.'

For Ben the sunlight dimmed even more as he recalled the dark enclosed space of the tunnel, the broad, fiercely whiskered head outlined against the distant doorway. 'How did you get him in then?' he asked fearfully.

'I talked to him a lot and coaxed him the way I did the others. It got easier as he learned to trust me.'

'Trust you?'

'Yes, when he realized I wasn't against him. He must feel like that about you too, or you'd never have got him back.'

He shook his head. 'It's different with me,' he said quietly.

'Why's that?'

'Raja hates me.'

A large eland doe had wandered to within metres of where they sat, her young calf thrusting at her teats, sucking noisily. The eyes of the mother were calm, placid, unconcerned by the nearness of the two human beings.

'Why should he hate you?' Ellie asked curiously.

'He knows what I'm like inside; what I'm capable of.'

Ellie nodded, the idea of Raja's being able to understand such things not sounding at all absurd to her. 'And what are you capable of?' she asked.

He remained silent for a while, biting at his lower lip, his teeth sinking painfully into the soft flesh. 'I had a dog once,' he began, and then regretted raising the subject.

'Yes?' she said encouragingly.

'He also found out what I was like,' he added, 'but only when it was too late.'

He thought that she would ask him more about the dog. Inwardly he prepared himself for the inevitable question. But all she said was, 'If Raja hates you, why did he let you cage him?'

'He had no choice.'

'How come?'

He plucked a blade of grass and tossed it into the air, the breeze quickly carrying it away.

'It's hard to explain,' he said, 'but there's a voice inside my head, that animals can hear. I used it to order him back.'

'You mean you forced him?' The same anxious frown, which he had first noticed in the moonlight, again creased the smooth skin of her forehead.

'Kind of, yes.'

'And is that the only way this voice works?'

'No. Other animals trust me when I Call to them. Raja's the only one who doesn't. I have to will him to do what I want.'

Ellie rocked forward onto her knees, bringing her face close to his. 'Then in future you'd better leave the tigers to me,' she said earnestly. 'You can cage some of the other cats.'

'Why should you take all the risks?' he answered, arguing with her even though the thought of never again having to face Raja filled him with relief.

'Because if you go on forcing him back to his cage, one of these nights he'll kill you.'

'Maybe.'

'No, not maybe.' She spoke now with quiet emphasis. 'I know him. In the end he'll kill you. That's for sure.'

He hesitated briefly before giving in. 'Yes, I suppose so.'

She smiled as though he were the one doing her a favour.

'All right, then, I keep the tigers for myself. Agreed?'

She held out her hand, but before he could take it the woman called Val came running towards them.

'You, Ben,' she called out, 'Molly wants you up at the admission building.'

'What for?'

Val's face, friendly until then, changed abruptly. 'Don't stand around asking questions!' she said angrily, fingering the rifle at her shoulder. 'Just do as you're told and get up there!'

Ben and Ellie crossed the wooden bridge spanning the ponds and approached the old admission building. Except for some peeling paint, the side facing into the Zoo was unchanged. A tall, pretentious structure, topped by an absurd dome, it reminded Ben, more even than the restaurant, of his childhood visits. Only the outer walls had been modified. As he climbed the steps, he could see through to where the arched entrance had been bricked up. Molly and Steve were waiting for him just inside the doors, in the reception area, an open space which had once housed the ticket office.

'You wanted me?' Ben asked.

Molly nodded, eyeing him speculatively, as if trying to gauge his usefulness. 'Steve and I have been discussing whether you're worth keeping,' she said bluntly.

'But you said he could stay!' Ellie interrupted, pushing past Ben.

'You shut your mouth!' Steve warned her, the animosity between them breaking out again.

Molly placed a steadying hand on his shoulder.

'I don't seem to remember you even being invited here, Ellie,' she said calmly. 'So if you want to stay, you'd better not speak out of turn.' She paused and turned back to Ben. 'Now where was I?' Acting absent-minded, she casually gathered a stray strand of blonde hair and tucked it behind her ear. 'Ah, yes, the problem of what to do with you. Steve here's of the opinion you aren't worth hanging on to. He doubts whether you could earn your keep, which after all is the main issue. What do you say to that?'

'I . . . I could help . . . ' he floundered, the question taking him by surprise.

'It's not enough to help,' Molly pointed out. 'I mean, Ellie's been doing the job on her own for quite a while. As Steve keeps reminding me, it's a waste to use two people where one will do. And waste, in these trying times, is something we can't afford.'

'But what if . . . ' Ben glanced covertly at Ellie, '. . . if something happened to one of us?'

'That thought did cross my mind last night,' she admitted. 'It's mainly why I let you go out there. I was curious to see if you'd cope on your own. But Steve's point still holds. We can't afford to keep two of everybody just in case. It's not economic. If Raja suddenly took it into his head to make a meal of Ellie . . . ' She smiled at the thought. 'Not that she'd make much of a meal! But *if* he did, then that'd be the time to look for a replacement. Not before. Don't you agree?'

He made no reply, desperately searching for reasons that would convince her of his worth. But he could think of nothing.

'Well?' she asked. And when he still remained silent: 'Really, I'm disappointed in you, Ben. I thought you'd do better than this in a crisis.' There was a disturbing suggestion of finality in her voice.

'Please,' he said, 'just let me stay for a while. See how things go.'

'Don't waste your time begging,' Ellie broke in coldly. 'They've got about as much pity as Raja. Less probably.'

Steve shook off Molly's detaining hand and took a half step forward. 'You're pushing your luck, Ellie,' he said. 'I wouldn't if I were you. We can always dump you and keep him. That's something I'd go for any day.'

90

Molly put her arm through Steve's and again drew him to her side. 'Now there's a suggestion!' she said, and smiled.

But Ellie, her eyes flashing angrily, was not easily intimidated. 'And here's another,' she retorted. 'We can both clear out and leave you to do your own dirty work!'

'Oh, come now, Ellie, there's no need to talk like that. I'd keep Ben if I could – if you'd show me how.'

Ellie grew abruptly calm, almost wary. 'But you already know why we need him.'

'Remind me.'

'What are you playing at, Molly?'

'Just remind me.'

'All right. The real danger time is dusk, when we've put one lot of animals away and haven't let the others go. Taronga's wide open then. Well, between us we can halve that danger time. While I'm freeing the cats on one side of the park, Ben can be doing the same on the other.'

'Which side of the park did you have in mind?'

Ellie's eyes narrowed. 'So that's what all this is about,' she said, the truth dawning on her. 'You want him to work with Raja. If he agrees, he can stay. Isn't that it?'

'It's possible.'

'But you saw him last night! What it cost him!'

Molly shrugged indifferently. 'I don't know about Ben's state of mind,' she said, 'but Steve and I have just come back from looking at Raja, and we've never seen him so upset before. Eight hours since he was locked up and he's still spitting fire. I like that. It's extra insurance for us because it means he's twice as dangerous. Now if Ben could guarantee to keep him in that state . . . '

'It's got nothing to do with Ben,' Ellie said quickly. 'It was the break-in that disturbed him.'

'He's usually calmer after a kill.'

'Last night was different.'

Molly switched her attention to Ben. 'What made the

difference last night?' she asked. 'Was it you?'

'Don't listen to her!' Ellie blurted out. 'She's trying to blackmail you.'

'No, not blackmail,' Molly said, still gazing directly at Ben. 'A choice, that's all.'

With an effort, Ben managed to return her gaze, looking straight into her cool, unfeeling eyes. 'I was the one who made Raja angry,' he said, unsure at first why he felt compelled to tell the truth.

'How did you do it?'

'It's the way I control him. He resents it.'

'So he'd stay angry if you worked with him?'

'I think so.'

'Well then, the choice is yours. Take him over and you earn yourself a place here.'

'There's another choice, Ben,' Ellie broke in. 'We can both leave Taronga. I'll go with you.'

He turned away from them all and looked out at the Zoo. He could see only the wooden bridge and the ponds with their backdrop of trees. Yet at that moment the whole of Taronga seemed to present itself to him. A complete world in miniature. Eden, he had called it. Hundreds of innocent animals, as yet unbetrayed, living peacefully in the midst of the city's chaos. Dependent for their safety not on human beings – not ultimately – but on a creature like themselves. Raja as their chief guardian; the key to their survival.

Behind him, Steve said in a jeering tone, 'I don't think he's got the guts to handle Raja.'

But it wasn't that which decided him. He turned back towards Molly. 'It's a deal. I'll cage Raja for you.'

'Good,' she murmured, but no longer smiling now that she had achieved her purpose.

Ellie, meanwhile, said nothing, remaining tight-lipped until they were outside, standing on the wooden bridge that spanned the ponds.

'You're a fool!' she said, the words bursting out of her. 'You fell for their stupid threats! You just let them bully you!'

'No,' he answered, 'it wasn't their threats that made up my mind.'

'What then?'

He gestured vaguely. 'This place. Taronga.'

Below them, a pair of black swans and a bedraggled-looking muscovy drake paddled slowly across the pond, their smooth, rounded breasts creating v-shaped patterns in the water.

'Taronga?' she asked incredulously. 'But you've only just got here. You don't know what it's really like.'

He was tempted, then, to try and explain it all to her: the reason for his decision; the necessity of putting himself at risk, of correcting the old imbalance, even though the thought of again confronting Raja made his heart jolt unpleasantly. But he merely said, 'I still think this place is worth fighting for.'

She shook her head. 'All you're doing is risking your life for Molly and Steve.'

'No, I'm not talking about the people,' he said. 'I know what they're like. It's the rest of it I want to preserve. The animals and the way they live. The fact that what's happened out there in the city hasn't affected them yet.'

'Hasn't it?'

'No, not yet. And we can keep it like that if we try.'

She shrugged, unwilling to go on arguing with him, and left the bridge, wandering off past the information centre. He caught up with her further along the path, at a point where they could look out over the trees towards the harbour and the distant high-rise buildings of the city.

'Taronga,' she murmured thoughtfully. 'D'you know what that means?' She gave him no chance to reply. 'It's an Aboriginal word meaning water views.'

The harbour, as he remembered it, no longer existed – the

ferries, the powerboats, the white splash of sails, all magically removed, leaving a wide expanse of intense blue. Yet beyond the water, the city centre retained its former aspect: the tower, the skyscrapers, the Opera House standing on the foreshore, all apparently untouched by time.

'Isn't it funny how it doesn't seem to change,' he said, indicating the distant skyline.

'It's like this place,' she answered. 'It only looks different when you get close and see what it's really like.' Almost as an afterthought, she added, 'Come on, I'll show you.'

She led him along the path to where one of the many telescopes, installed for the benefit of visitors, still stared out into space. The original coin-slot and time-mechanism had been removed, leaving the lenses unobscured.

'Here,' she said, swinging it round, 'take a look.'

He peered through the eye-piece and immediately the city leaped towards him. There was nothing timeless about it now, the illusion of permanence shattered by the prevailing air of ruin and decay. It was apparent in everything he saw: the steelwork of the bridge streaked with rust; tiles missing from the shell-shapes of the Opera House; the upper storeys of the skyscrapers almost windowless. The whole distant scene speaking to him of sadness and loss.

He straightened up. 'What went wrong?' he asked. 'They said it wasn't going to affect us. It was all up there, in the northern hemisphere. We were supposed to be the lucky ones, who'd escaped. That's what they said on the radio and telly. I heard them.'

'They made a mistake,' she said.

'Yes, but why did it happen? It didn't have to. Not to us.'

'I think it had something to do with being cut off. The way we are here in Taronga. Everything just went bad after that.'

'But this isn't bad,' he objected. 'The animals are still alive. They're even freer than they used to be.'

She smiled, a trace of disbelief in her expression, and

suddenly he had the feeling that there was something she wasn't telling him.

'Well aren't they?' he asked.

But she evaded the question. 'Even if what you say is true, how long d'you think it can last? Sooner or later one of the break-ins'll be successful.'

'So what?' he answered defensively. 'You can't tell me the people outside are trying to wreck the place. They want it for themselves. Isn't that right?'

She nodded.

'Well then, Taronga will go on the same as before. Nothing will really change. Not for the animals anyway.'

But again she shied away from giving him a definite answer. 'Maybe,' she muttered vaguely, her voice, her face, registering the same uncertainty; her eyes fixed on the sad outline of the deserted city.

CHAPTER TEN

His nightly ordeal, if anything, proved to be worse than he had anticipated. It began each evening at dusk when, with all the other animals locked away, he went alone to the now familiar row of cages. They housed not only tigers, but also leopards, jaguars, and a pair of sleek-coated pumas. He released them one pair at a time, Calling to them gently, coaxing them out into the darkening tunnel. With a low growl of welcome, they would come padding towards him, blinking in the fading evening light, their subtle markings and the soft texture of their coats already blending into the advancing shadows. Cage by cage, he worked his way along the line, reaching the tigers last of all.

Ranee, now that she had accepted him, offered no resistance. Often, as she glided out into the open, she would purposely raise her head and allow the side of her muzzle to brush against his hand where it gripped the side of the opening.

'Good girl,' he would murmur softly, encouraging her to follow the other cats towards the far doorway.

Raja always came last of all. Torn between his longing for the open spaces of Taronga and his hatred of the figure standing between him and partial freedom, he would linger sullenly at the back of the cage, his long striped body swinging to and fro in agitation.

'Come,' Ben would order him, wincing as he made contact with the savage mind, and Raja would stalk forward, teeth bared.

Getting him into the tunnel was only the first step. Like Ben, he was loath to turn from his adversary and he would give ground grudgingly, snarling as he backed away. Invariably, that slow nightly retreat developed into a kind of duel: with Ben holding the tiger at bay by sheer strength of will, his silent commands acting as a protective shield; and Raja constantly seeking for a weak point in that shield through which he could tear at his enemy.

It was a relief to both of them when they reached the outer door. Sensing the open spaces behind him, Raja would whirl around and leap off into the encroaching night. And Ben, dazed and trembling, would suddenly find himself alone, the bond holding him to the tiger abruptly severed. He would stand quite still, listening, knowing what must follow. A few moments would pass and then, with a force and energy that always took him by surprise, Raja's triumphant peal of freedom would sweep silently over the hillside. It no longer sounded alluring. For Ben it had become a deeply disturbing cry, a rejection of all restraint, which seemed to claw at the stars and grope yearningly for the vast inland areas of the continent, as though claiming them for itself.

With Raja roaming Taronga at will, Ben had to be extra careful, constantly on the lookout for a surprise attack as he stole back up to the restaurant or crossed the park to the house overlooking the harbour, which was where Ellie stayed.

Only once did he make the mistake of thinking that, with Raja released, the most testing part of his evening task was over. As he stepped through the outer door into the peace and tranquillity of the soft evening light, he relaxed his guard: and Raja, watching from the bushes, too filled with hatred to wait for a better opportunity, burst from cover and leaped towards him. Fortunately for Ben, there was an expanse of open hillside around the cages, and although he was startled he had time to stop the charge, his stern rejection rocking the animal back onto its haunches. Nevertheless, he recognized the incident for what it was – a warning – and from then on he took more care, pausing at every shadow or sign of movement, sustaining his protective shield until he reached safety.

Raja also learned from that incident. He was never again so hasty. Using all his natural cunning, he took to waiting for Ben in the most unlikely places: on the roof of the elephant house, his broad, whiskered face peering over the mock-Indian parapet; in the dusky interior of the rotunda, close to the restaurant; once, even in the shadow of the restaurant itself, his striped form rearing up as Ben approached the door.

Yet those evening confrontations, although nerve-racking, were as nothing compared with the nightly ritual of Calling the animals back into captivity. Just before dawn Ben would pack hunks of meat into a plastic bag and creep warily down to the cages. All the cats except Raja would come at his bidding, loping in through the open door, attracted partly by his Call and partly by the scent of raw meat. He would lock each of the cages in turn and then, with the one remaining piece of meat, go in search of Raja.

Usually he found him near the lower fence where, according to Ellie, most of his kills had been made. Down there on a still night it was possible to hear the harbour waters washing against the shore, and Ben often wondered whether that sound, with its associations of restlessness and freedom, also attracted the tiger. But when he probed the darkness, searching for the secret longings which lay beneath the surface of Raja's mind, he met only an impenetrable barrier of hostility.

Night after night he tried to break down that barrier. Standing on the lower path, he would make coaxing noises, crooning soothing words into the black, pre-dawn hush. But it never had any effect. Always, eventually, he had to enter the thick bush and seek out the face of his enemy, searching for those familiar striped markings which, by day, stood out like fire, but here in the darkness were indistinguishable from the surrounding shadows. He would locate them at last, and once again their minds would lock onto each other, that bitter combat, which had become their only means of communication, beginning anew.

It ended in the same way every morning: with Ben, pale and exhausted, hurling the joint of meat into the cage; and with Raja, after a last vengeful swipe at the empty air, sidling in after it. Thankfully, Ben would slide the door down and fasten it with the padlock – yet always in the sure knowledge that nothing had been achieved. If anything, they had merely moved a step closer to that fatal moment when he, Ben, either through fatigue or desperation, would be caught unawares.

He had no real doubt that such a moment awaited him, though he tried hard not to think about it. Walking out into the grey light of early dawn, the keys to the padlocks hanging from his belt, he thought instead of a time when, hopefully, habit alone would render his ordeal more bearable. Tomorrow, he assured himself, it would be easier. But it never was. As the nights slipped by and the strain began to tell, each confrontation became more daunting than the last. Raja's patterned face, its beauty and its deadliness inseparable, gradually came to haunt him, rarely absent from his mind for long. It seemed always to be there in the background, no matter where he was or what he was doing, a shadowy image lurking at the edge of his daylight existence, stealing even into his sleep.

Soon, finding it impossible to rest at night, he took to sleeping in the mornings, lying out on the open hillside or in the shade of a tree. Yet still Raja's face pursued him. Except that in his dreams it frequently became confused with the

99

head of the dying dingo, the staring eyes of both animals merging into the softer brown eyes of the dog. 'Run!' he would murmur, tossing feverishly from side to side. 'Run!' But the face only drew nearer, blurring out of focus, the long yellowish fangs reaching for him vengefully. And with a cry that was as much an utterance of grief as of fear, he would start awake, his body drenched in sweat, his face and neck hot and clammy.

On one such morning he woke to find Ellie sitting beside him.

'How long do you think you can carry on like this?' she asked quietly.

He sat up, rubbing his eyes. 'As long as I have to.'

She placed a dark hand on his. 'If you don't stop, you know how it's going to end.'

He nodded, his dream still too vividly present for any easy denials.

'So why go on?' she pressed him.

'I've told you,' he answered gruffly, 'I have to.'

'Have to? Just because Molly says so?'

'No, that's not the main reason.'

'Then why?'

'Because . . . ' – he hesitated.

'Is it because of what happened before? You mentioned something about a dog once. Is that it?'

'Partly.'

'What else?'

'It's too complicated to explain.'

'Try, Ben, please.' She was coaxing him now as if he were one of the reluctant animals.

'It started with a bloke called Greg,' he said, forcing the words out one by one. 'That was in the bush, out west. The two of us used to hunt together, for roos mainly. Greg was the one with the gun. My job . . . '

'Go on,' she urged him gently.

100

Slowly, hesitantly, often breaking off for minutes at a time, he told her about the two years he had spent with Greg, ending with a brief outline of the events leading up to the death of the dog. She listened attentively, her legs drawn up against her body, both thin arms curled about her knees. When he had finished she said nothing for a while, the two of them sitting quietly together, the even whir of cicadas accentuating the silence. Immediately below them, a shy, delicately stepping gazelle lifted its head and looked in their direction, its mouth moving rhythmically as it chewed.

'So now you're trying to make up for what happened before,' she said finally.

Stated like that, it sounded so simple that he wondered why he had not seen it as clearly himself.

'Yes,' he admitted, 'I suppose so.'

'But you can't, Ben. Not here.'

'Why not?'

'Because it's as rotten as everywhere else.'

'You keep saying that,' he reminded her, 'but you never really explain what's wrong with it.'

She ran the pink tip of her tongue nervously around her lips. 'It's . . . it's where it's all leading,' she said uncertainly.

'And where's that?'

She shook her head. 'Talking about it won't change anything.'

'Change what, for God's sake?'

She glanced aside, taking refuge in the same evasiveness she had used once before. 'I've never lived in the bush the way you have,' she said, speaking quickly so he wouldn't interrupt. 'I'm like my mum – we were both brought up in Sydney. Mum came from out Parramatta way. But not dad. He grew up in the Territory.'

'I don't see,' he broke in, but she cut him short.

'I asked him once how Aboriginals – the ones who still live in the old ways – thought about animals in the bush. D'you

101

know what he said?'

'Go on.'

'He said they thought of them as equals. Not human beings on one side and animals on the other, but all of them sharing the land together.'

'They still used animals as food,' Ben objected.

'Yes, that worried me for a while. But then I read something in a book. Not about Aboriginals – about some other tribal people somewhere. It said that before they ate meat, they begged the animal they'd killed to forgive them. I asked dad if that was what he meant.'

'And was it?'

'I'm not sure. He just mumbled something about it being too late for forgiveness. Last Days had begun then, and like most people he was pretty depressed. Ships had stopped coming to Australia and no planes had landed for weeks. Everything was breaking down. It was already dangerous to go into the streets, even in daylight. It's too late for forgiveness – that's all he'd say.'

'I still don't see what any of ... ' Ben stopped, suddenly aware of what she was trying to tell him. 'All this forgiveness stuff,' he added more slowly, 'you're talking about me and Raja, aren't you?'

She turned her dark eyes towards him. 'In a way.'

'You're saying he'll never learn to see me as a friend, to treat me the way he treats you.'

'Not in here he won't.'

'What's Taronga got to do with it?'

'Everything.'

He stood up impatiently. 'The way you go on about this place,' he said, 'anyone'd think it was hell on earth. Well I've got news for you: compared with what's happening on the other side of that fence, this is paradise. Eden. That's what I called it the first day I spent here. Remember? And I wasn't joking.'

102

She leaned back, gazing up at him, the sunlight gilding the smooth, silky skin of her face and bare shoulders. 'Is that the way you feel about Taronga when you're face to face with Raja?' she asked quietly. 'Does it still feel like paradise?'

The question was like a physical blow, catching him off guard. 'No . . . not then.'

'Well what you see when you're looking into Raja's eyes – that's the truth about Taronga. Raja understands this place, what it's really like, underneath, the same as he understands about you.'

'But he can't think like us,' Ben protested.

'He doesn't have to. He relies on his feelings. They tell him all he needs to know. And what they tell him – well, you've seen it in his eyes, haven't you? How it's too late for forgiveness here too. Because Taronga's not a place to hide in, Ben. It's just a great big cage, and what went wrong in the rest of Sydney is already locked in here, waiting to go wrong again.'

'It'll never be like those streets out there!' he said desperately, backing away from her. 'I won't let it happen.'

'I don't see how you can stop it. You're no freer than the animals. You just do as you're told, the same as them. Molly gives all the orders around here because she has the guns to back her up. She's the one with the power. The kind of power that wrecked Sydney. And one of these days she's going to use it.'

Her dark, troubled eyes had ceased to look at him. She was staring out over the treetops towards the wide, untrammelled spaces of the harbour.

'What will she do?' Ben asked, all his objections momentarily stilled by the quiet conviction in her voice.

She turned towards him, a thin beaded line of perspiration showing on her upper lip. 'Molly's not the kind of person to keep you waiting,' she said. 'You'll find out, if Raja lets you live long enough.'

That same day, in the early part of the afternoon, Molly called a special meeting of all the people in the Zoo. They gathered in the large, formal dining area at the end of the restaurant, its doors and windows open to the light and air. Molly, with Steve beside her, stood on a chair to address the gathering, her back to the windows so that only her dark silhouette could be seen clearly.

Ben, in the midst of the crowd, looked about him at the many upturned faces. He now knew all of them by sight. In many ways they reminded him of Chas's men, the ones he had seen in the front room of the house. They had the same grim set to their mouths, the same vaguely unpleasant expressions. Not that that was surprising. These were, after all, the survivors. But surviving for what? What purpose?

His train of thought was interrupted by Molly as she started to speak.

'I won't keep you here long,' she said, 'because I know you all have a lot to do. But I thought I'd better bring you up to date with what's going on. As most of you probably realize, there's been quite a lot of activity around Taronga recently. Just to be on the safe side, for the past few nights I've sent small patrols over the wire to check out the Mosman area. What they found isn't too good from our point of view. But Steve here was on those patrols, so I'll let him tell you the rest.'

She indicated that Steve should step forward, though she remained on the chair, looming above them, her shadowy outline etched sharply against the outside brightness.

'Not counting the past few nights,' Steve began, 'it must be six months or more since I went over the wire. Things were quiet then – just a few deros and one small gang. Well it's not like that now. The word must be out that Taronga's where the tucker is, because they're coming in from everywhere. Most of them are half-starved and pretty run-down, but the numbers alone make them dangerous. We had trouble

104

finding a street that didn't have people skulking around in it. They didn't bother us any. As soon as they spotted us, they ran off. In a few weeks' time, though, who knows? My guess is that they'll start getting organized. The gang out there that's always given us aggro might even recruit some of them.'

'And then what?' someone in the crowd asked.

It was Molly who answered. 'If we've got any brains, we don't let things reach that stage. At the moment they're just like flies buzzing aimlessly round the honey pot. Now's the time to act.'

'You mean we swat some of them?' the same voice called out.

There was widespread laughter.

'Precisely,' Molly replied, no hint of amusement in her voice. 'We thin them out – cull them, the way we do the animals here in the Zoo when the numbers get out of hand.'

All around Ben, young men and women were nodding in agreement, many of them smiling at the prospect. The woman called Val, standing only a few paces away, raised her clenched fist in a kind of salute. Ben, unnerved by the sudden change of feeling in the room, glanced round at Ellie, but her smooth dark face was closed, telling him nothing.

'I'm glad to see you approve,' Molly added, as more and more fists were raised, the arms stiff and straight, pointing towards her. 'The best thing we can do is send a good-sized raiding party out right away; clean the whole area up before anything starts. If any of you would like to volunteer, stay behind and see me now.'

She stepped down from the chair and immediately most of those present began pushing forward, eager to be chosen.

'What about me, Molly?' voices called out.

'You can count me in.'

'Time we had a bit of sport.'

For Ben, the atmosphere in the room had become stifling, and he ducked and weaved his way through the crowd towards the door. Outside, on the empty pathway, with the warm sunlight falling gently on his bare head, he felt free again, the air clean and untainted. He thought at first that he was alone, but then Ellie appeared unexpectedly beside him.

'D'you still think it's all that different from outside?' she asked.

He turned away and began walking rapidly along a path that led across the hillside. He could hear Ellie's footsteps close behind, but he didn't look back – passing the large seal pools, empty now, the blue paint peeling away in shreds; stopping only when he reached a secluded grassy slope. A small flock of sheep, once part of the children's farm section of the Zoo, were grazing peacefully, not even lifting their heads at his approach.

'You can't run away in Taronga,' Ellie reminded him. 'It's too small.'

He turned to face her. 'What else do you expect Molly to do?' he said belligerently. 'Wait until all those people out there are hammering on the gates? It's them or us.'

'That's what everyone was saying at the start of Last Days,' Ellie reminded him. 'And look what happened.'

'But surely we have the right to defend ourselves,' he answered, the argument sounding hollow even in his own ears.

'Defence?' she said scornfully. 'Is that what you call sending an armed raiding party into the streets?'

'All right, it's aggression. I admit that. Why d'you think I cleared out of there so fast? But honestly, Ellie, what alternative do we have?'

He could tell by the promptness of her reply that it was a question she had thought a lot about.

'Molly could try helping some of those people,' she said, 'maybe even expand Taronga a bit. That's our only real hope: to make Taronga bigger and bigger, until everyone's inside. Keeping most of them out won't work.'

'D'you really think Molly would consider doing something like that?'

She shook her head. 'No. That's why I think this place is hopeless.'

But he couldn't bring himself to accept that part of her argument. 'And yet you stay here,' he put in quickly, trying to catch her unawares. 'If it's so hopeless, why don't you push off?'

'It's mainly the cats that keep me here,' she said simply. She paused and looked candidly at Ben. 'And what's your reason for staying?'

'You already know that,' he answered, speaking just a little too quickly. 'Never mind about Molly – Taronga itself is worth preserving. The animals have a future here, even if we don't. They must have!'

He had intended to sound confident, convinced, but his voice carried a ring of desperation, as if responding to the small nagging doubt that had arisen in his mind. He wasn't wholly sure where that doubt had come from. And when he tried to trace it to its source, all he could think of was the recent gathering in the restaurant: the stiff-armed salutes; the young men and women surging forward, eager to act as Molly's volunteers.

CHAPTER ELEVEN

The raiding party slipped over the fence near the upper entrance as soon as it was dark. Not long afterwards the distant, sporadic gunfire began. Ben was alone in the upstairs of the restaurant when the first shot rang out and he ran to the window; but there was nothing to be seen, the night far too dark, the sound coming from over the swell of the hillside. For an hour or more he remained crouched by the window, listening, the shots sometimes stopping for a while and then breaking out again – the sharp, staccato noise of repeater rifles cracking ominously in the background. Once there was a dull, muffled explosion, like a deep booming within the hillside, and a burst of orange-yellow light stained a small section of the sky. It was followed, in the restaurant below him, by cheers and laughter, and someone began singing 'Advance Australia Fair' in a raucous voice.

Leaving his room, he stole quietly down the stairs. A group of people were sitting in a circle on the floor, passing a bottle between them. One of them, the man called Terry, spotted Ben.

'Come on, join the celebration,' he called, his words accompanied by another sustained crackle of rifle fire. 'Hear that? We're really giving it to them tonight. Not before bloody time. Teach the bastards to come nosing round here.' He held the bottle out towards Ben, his close-set eyes looking dull and slightly out of focus even in the lamplight.

'Not right now, thanks,' Ben said, backing away, trying to disguise his feelings of distaste. 'I just thought I'd nick out and check on the animals. Make sure the noise isn't upsetting them too much.'

'Suit yourself.'

He drew back the lock and slipped outside, pulling the door closed behind him. A second explosion lit the sky, and somewhere near by the roar of what sounded like a lion was raised in excited anticipation. Ben knew why: all the predators had learned to associate the noise of firearms with the immediate prospect of food. That was not so with the more timid animals. When he opened his mind to the rest of Taronga, the night suddenly came alive with the cries of terrified creatures. Moved by pity, Ben sent out a low, wide-ranging Call, trying to reassure them. Under less testing circumstances his silent appeal might have had some effect, but now it was all but lost in the general clamour of alarm.

Frustrated by his own uselessness, Ben checked that Raja was not in the vicinity and then ran silently across the park to the house on the far side. Ellie opened the door, ushering him inside.

Here too a group of young people were celebrating, cheering after each outbreak of firing.

'About time we carried the fight to them,' someone shouted in a drunken voice.

'Yes, clear the garbage off the streets.'

In tight-lipped silence, Ellie led him to her room at the back of the house. A heavy blind covered the window and a single candle was burning in the middle of the floor.

'What's it like over at your place?' she asked. She looked tense and hollow-eyed.

'About the same as here.'

'And the animals? How are they taking it?'

'Scared stiff, most of them. Not the cats though. They're just over-excited.'

She nodded. 'Yes, I thought so.'

But he could tell that for the moment it wasn't the plight of the animals that was concerning her. Her mind was clearly elsewhere, imagining those overgrown, darkened streets beyond the fence.

'How long d'you reckon this will go on?' he asked.

'Hard to say. It's never happened before so I can't tell.' She paused, and then said angrily, 'I warned you about Molly, didn't I? What she's really like!'

'The rest are just as bad. She couldn't do it on her own.'

'Maybe, but it was her idea. Hunting down a lot of deros as if they're animals! No, less than animals! As if they're insects or something!'

He tried to take her hand, to placate her, but she snatched it away. 'Well this is the price you have to pay for Taronga!' she went on bitterly. 'D'you still think it's worth it?'

'It'll soon be over,' he murmured, but even to himself that sounded a foolish remark.

'Over? Is something like this ever over?' A third dull explosion rumbled across the hillside. 'Listen to them!' she said, holding up one warning finger. 'Using hand-grenades on a few half-starved scarecrows who only want to escape anyway. And thinking of it as fun! People like that don't care how far they go. I'm telling you, for Molly it's just a beginning.'

'But once the streets are cleared . . . ' he protested.

'That's just the point,' she interrupted him hotly, 'they'll never be cleared. All the time there's food in here people will keep coming. This – what you can hear now, maybe worse – will go on for as long as Taronga exists.'

He said nothing to that, the two of them sitting miserably side by side, trying not to visualize the grim reality which lay behind the distant noise. It went on hour after hour as the

110

raiding party worked its way systematically along the streets.

At one point, after a protracted burst of firing, Ellie muttered angrily, 'Remember what she called it? Thinning them out! Culling them!'

But when Ben still didn't answer, she fell silent; finally resting her head on his shoulder and falling into a troubled, murmurous sleep.

In the early hours of the morning Ben also began to doze, his whole body jerking involuntarily whenever the firing broke out anew. He dreamed, briefly, that he was back home with his parents. They were standing outside their house, watching a fireworks display. Rockets were being launched from the distant cliffs, exploding high above the sea and descending in a shower of livid sparks. 'What's it all for?' he kept asking anxiously. 'It's Australia Day,' his mother replied. But even in his dream he knew that wasn't the right answer. One rocket, much brighter than the rest, arched above him and disintegrated, throwing out a single brilliant star which floated down and landed at his feet. As it struck the ground it turned into a flickering plume of fire which gradually resolved itself into the flame-like markings of Raja. The huge head was so close that he could see the starlight and the sparks from the descending rockets reflected in the fiercely staring eyes. Then the heavy paw had him, and as he struggled to break free he awoke and found that Ellie was shaking him gently.

'It's nearly dawn,' she whispered. 'Time we were moving.'

He staggered groggily to his feet. There was very little noise from the raiding party now, just an occasional shot puncturing the silence.

'If you like,' Ellie suggested, 'I can see to Raja. No one'll find out.'

It was a tempting offer, but he shook his head. 'No, he'll be hard to handle after all the disturbance. I'll see to him.'

It took them only a few minutes to collect some rank meat

111

stored in the laundry. Then, picking their way between the bodies sprawled on the living-room floor, they let themselves out into the park. Although dawn was not far off, it was still pitch black, the sky heavily overcast.

'Good luck,' Ellie whispered, and slid away, her dark skin dissolving into the surrounding shadows.

With his usual caution, Ben made first for the line of cages on the opposite side of the park. Most of the cats, frustrated by the fruitless hours of conflict, were already there waiting for him, eager enough to accept his offer of food and creep into their familiar places of refuge. That left only Raja – and as always he was lingering down near the bottom fence.

It was impossible to see him in the intense blackness, and Ben approached with special care, fully expecting him to be more angry and dangerous than usual. But even Raja was subdued – confused by the way the gunfire had gone on and on while the hillside had remained as empty of human activity as on any normal night. And although he let out a low growl of defiance, he too was ready to return to the less bewildering security of the cages.

Yet he didn't simply follow Ben. At the first silent word of command he backed away, responding to the Call as if it were another fruitless burst of gunfire. Nothing like that had ever happened before and Ben immediately sensed the reason for it: Raja had always associated him with the rest of humanity, seen him as representative of the whole hated species. Now, understandably, he saw Ben as the source of his present confusion – the cause of this new kind of noise which could somehow disrupt the night without satisfying his need to hunt and eat.

As Ben realized at once, it was too good an opportunity to miss. Instead of hurrying Raja back to his cage, he waited, holding him there as the minutes slipped by. A tinge of grey gradually appeared in the blackness beneath the trees, Raja's head and shoulders showing dimly against the background

112

foliage. At last, from far over the hill, there came a ragged crackle of shots, and straight away Ben opened his mind to the animal crouched only a few paces away. The effect was unmistakable – Raja throwing up his head in astonishment as he detected not the harsh voice of command, but a frustration similar to his own; those distant, pointless spurts of noise as alien to Ben as to himself. His astonishment lasted only for a moment, but for that brief space of time their minds ceased to be locked in unforgiving combat. They seemed to brush against each other, gently, a suggestion of understanding passing between them.

It was gone almost instantly, Raja once again backing resentfully up the slope, the battle of wills continuing as before. Yet Ben had no doubt that for the first time they had made real contact. And when, ten minutes later, he withdrew the key from the padlock on Raja's cage, he experienced a surge of genuine elation.

Walking back down the tunnel, he gazed raptly out into the fading darkness. The shadowy outline of Taronga had never appeared more beautiful to him, the dawning day, the dewy freshness of the air, like a new beginning. Again he savoured that brief moment of understanding. For all its brevity it was something which, with care and patience, he could build upon. Develop. Given time, he thought contentedly, anything was possible. Anything.

But at that point his train of thought was interrupted by a last rumbling explosion – a low warning growl, far more savage than any sound Raja could make, shuddering through the whole hillside.

The raiding party returned later that morning. Ben didn't see them arrive because he was given the task of turning off the electric current while they climbed over the fence, but from his place at the switchboard behind the restaurant he heard cheers of welcome. By the time he had restored the power

113

and run to the front, they were already trooping down the main pathway, looking tired but pleased with themselves. Steve was leading them, his face blackened by smoke, his rifle sloped casually across one shoulder. In his free hand he held a stout length of cord that was looped around the necks of two ragged figures, a man and a woman, shuffling along behind. At first Ben thought they were old – their faces haggard and lined, their bodies bent forward – but as they passed him he saw they were merely dirty and half-starved, their eyes gleaming feverishly.

'Who are they?' he asked Ellie who had sidled up beside him.

'Prisoners,' she answered shortly.

'What do they want them for?'

'I expect Molly's got her reasons.'

Those reasons became apparent early that afternoon when Ben and Ellie, sitting in the shade of the rotunda, first heard the cries. They were muffled to begin with, but soon grew louder: cries of pain mostly, with an undertone of protest.

'What's going on?' Ben asked.

He and Ellie approached the restaurant and looked inside. The two ragged figures were tied to chairs, the eyes of the man already puffy and half-closed. Steve was standing over them, Molly lounging in the background.

'Ask him again,' Molly said nonchalantly.

Steve raised his fist and Ellie, reacting faster than Ben, raced across the room and clutched at his arm.

'Stop it!' she shouted, clinging on to him.

He tore himself free and struck out at her, sending her crashing back against the front windows, a fleck of blood in the corner of her mouth. 'You've been asking for this, Ellie!' he said threateningly.

'No, Steve!' Molly called out sharply. 'I won't have any fighting amongst ourselves!' And then in a reasonable tone which revealed just a hint of anger, 'You shouldn't push your nose into things you don't understand, Ellie.'

'I can understand what's going on here!' she answered hotly. 'Anybody could.'

'Yes, but he's doing it for a purpose. Last night he ran into pockets of resistance, some of it organized. We've got to find out how widespread that organization is. That's why Steve brought these two back: they could have the kind of information we need.'

'But they don't know anything!' Ben protested, crossing the room and standing beside Ellie.

'What makes you so sure of that?' Molly flashed out, some of her suppressed anger beginning to show.

'You only have to look at them! At the state they're in! They're more like hunted animals than human beings!'

'They'd still kill you given the chance.'

'That's because they're starving and desperate. You don't have that excuse, Molly. And nor does Steve.'

The full force of Molly's anger came boiling to the surface, two livid spots appearing just below her cheekbones. 'That's enough!' she shouted. 'I'm giving you two kids exactly thirty seconds to get out of here!'

'It'll still be pointless,' he insisted, 'whether we're here or not.'

'Thirty seconds!' she repeated.

'And if we refuse to go?' he answered defiantly.

'Then tonight,' she hissed at him, 'when Raja's fed, you'll be the meat in his cage!'

He could tell from the look on her face that it was no idle threat.

'Come on,' Ellie urged, tugging him towards the door.

'But we can't . . . !' he said, aware that the eyes of the two bound figures were gazing at him imploringly.

'She means it, Ben. Come on.'

He trailed miserably outside, feeling cowardly and useless.

'It's like I told you,' Ellie advised him. 'Molly's the power around here. Once she makes up her mind, there's nothing anyone can do to stop her.'

'And the prisoners?' he asked.

'Let's hope she sees sense and doesn't give Steve a free hand with them.'

For the remainder of the afternoon they stayed as far from the restaurant as possible, whiling away the hours in the vicinity of the weatherboard house where Ellie spent the nights. Not until darkness had fallen and the cats were released from their cages did Ben return to the restaurant. As he stepped in through the front entrance, Steve, hearing the soft click of the lock, called to him, 'The cats out yet?'

'My lot are. Ellie's should be out by now too.'

'Right, give me a hand here.'

Ben went over to where Steve was untying the two prisoners. The man's face was badly battered, the woman's mouth swollen and bleeding.

'Have you finished with them?' he asked, plucking at the knot which bound the woman's hands.

'You could put it that way,' Steve answered vaguely.

'What'll you do with them now?'

'I'll show you.' As the last rope fell away, Steve grabbed them both by the scruff of the neck and dragged them to the door. 'Time for your constitutional,' he said with a grin.

Before Ben fully realized what was happening, Steve had yanked open the door and pitched them both out into the darkness.

'No, wait!' Ben half shouted, lunging forward just as the door swung closed.

'Molly's orders,' Steve told him, still with the grin on his face.

Ben said nothing, Ellie's words of that afternoon coming back to him with renewed force: 'Molly's the power around here. Once she makes up her mind . . .' Yes, Ellie was right – he knew that. It was futile trying to defy Molly openly. If he

116

was going to oppose her, he would have to revert to more devious methods.

'Oh well, if Molly says so,' he muttered, struggling to keep his voice under control, 'then I suppose it must be all right.'

To his amazement, Steve took his agreement at its face value. 'You're learning, Kid,' he responded approvingly, and wandered off towards the far end of the building.

For the moment Ben was alone in the cafeteria section. Quickly, he ducked around the corner to the counter where the telephone was kept. He knew the code that he wanted – three long rings – and he spun the handle rapidly, pausing between each ring. A man's voice answered.

'That you, Molly?'

'No, it's Ben. Can I speak to Ellie?'

The voice took on a guarded, suspicious tone. 'Molly's the only one supposed to use that phone.'

'I know, but she gave me permission. She's . . . er . . . she's busy right now.'

A brief hesitation. 'Yes, well I suppose that's okay then. Hold on.'

Ellie came to the phone soon afterwards. 'Ben?'

'Listen!' he whispered urgently. 'The two prisoners have just been kicked outside. They won't have a hope on their own. Can you hold the cats on your side of the park?'

'I'll try.'

'Good, but you'll have to be quick.'

The phone immediately went dead and Ben replaced the receiver. Walking slowly now, so as not to attract attention, he made for the door. Nobody called out or asked him where he was going, and seconds later he too was outside in the darkness.

There was no sign of the two prisoners, but a brief probing Call alerted him to hunting activity further down the slope. He began running as fast as he could, leaping down flights of steps, looking frantically about him as he followed the twists and turns of the path. Not until he was somewhere below the elephant house did he catch sight of them: standing huddled together beside a public shelter, the sinister shape of a leopard barring their way.

'No!' he Called silently, following the command with a strong danger signal.

Baffled, the leopard sidled uneasily around the two figures, though still within striking distance.

'Don't move!' Ben warned them.

But at the sound of his voice they panicked completely, the woman running wildly off through the trees, the man heading in the general direction of the lower fence. It was impossible for Ben to follow them straight away. Putting himself between the leopard and the two fleeing figures, he again signalled extreme danger: and reluctantly, hissing in protest, the animal turned and loped away up the hillside. Only then did Ben continue down the path.

The woman, at that stage, could have been anywhere: her whereabouts was something he would have to determine later. His most pressing task was to save the man from Raja. Sprinting for all he was worth, he reached the lower path, his mind open, searching the darkness below. Within seconds he located Raja – that characteristic wall of silence excluding him – and simultaneously heard a sobbing cry of fear. He didn't hesitate, crashing down through the bush, forcing his way between shrubs and trees, skidding and nearly falling on the steeply sloping ground. Even so, he was only just in time: the man flattened against the wall in the speckled moonlight, his battered face further disfigured by abject terror; and only a few paces away, crouched and ready to spring, the long deathly shape of Raja.

'Get back!' Ben commanded silently.

For once those fiery eyes were not turned on him: they remained fixed on the cringing figure of the man, the great shoulder and thigh muscles knotted in anticipation.

Exerting all his mental strength, Ben willed the tiger away. For a full minute nothing happened, the night completely silent except for the man's quick gasping breaths. Then, grudgingly, Raja began to draw back, his eyes fixed burningly on the exposed throat of his prey.

Without any slackening of concentration, Ben said softly, 'I can't hold him for long. Get out of here while you have the chance.'

But the man was too petrified to obey, his hands groping ineffectually at the wall behind him – that small movement rousing Raja anew, making him stir restlessly.

'For God's sake!' Ben almost shouted, straining now to maintain control. 'If you want to stay alive, get over that wall!'

The man blinked several times, as though suddenly coming awake; and Raja, perhaps sensing that his prey was about to escape, snarled menacingly. It was that low guttural sound which drove the man to action. Whirling around, he clambered up onto the wall and began forcing his way through the strands of wire, the barbed knots scoring deep scratches in his hands and arms.

'Hurry!' Ben urged him.

The man's head and shoulders were already through, his body squirming frantically as he tried to break free of the clutching spikes. 'Help me!' he cried plaintively. 'You have to help me!'

Ben would have gone to him if he could, but Raja, maddened by the scent of blood, was snarling and lashing out wildly at the constricting darkness.

'You're nearly there,' Ben shouted, 'just a bit further!'

While the man struggled, Ben made a final effort to keep Raja back, focussing all his energy on that one task, forgetting in his singleness of purpose that Raja was not the only threat lurking within Taronga. And at that moment, Ranee, skulking unnoticed in the nearby bushes, leaped out into the open and struck.

It was all over in a second. A single blow on the upper portion of the spine and the man hung lifelessly from the wire, his face, mercifully, sunk in shadow. Ben, far too late, turned shocked eyes towards him; and Raja, taking advantage of his lapse in concentration, also leaped forward. Not to strike at Ben, but merely to claim his portion of the prey: the two animals pawing at the ragged, doll-like body and the pitifully thin legs.

Ben stumbled away, unable to watch, scrambling back up towards the path. In his shocked state he remained there for a minute or two as if dazed, no longer sure of what he should do next; and it was only a distant cry which reminded him of the woman.

Almost automatically he began running again, following the curving line of the lower fence, the path he was on sloping down towards the old exit building. He could see the woman now, darting desperately to and fro, from one end of the building to the other, unaware that it offered her no escape – the main archway long since closed off, the tall metal turnstiles welded into place. As he sprinted down the slope he also spotted Ellie, a slight, dark figure standing in the middle of the path, not far from the woman, yet making no effort to go to her. He didn't understand that at first, why she should be standing quite so still. Only when he drew closer, when he could see her more clearly – the way she had turned her back on the exit and was staring into the shadows – did he understand what was happening. This time, however, he had no opportunity to react. Before he could Call, a heavily maned lion charged from cover: leaping across the open space, the animal brushed Ellie aside and pounced upon the woman, dragging her down. There was a short high-pitched scream, choked off almost before it had begun; and then, barely audible above the sound of Ben's rapid footsteps, a long rumbling growl.

'Ellie!' Ben shouted, fearing that she too was dead.

To his relief, she rose unsteadily to her feet.

'You all right?' he asked breathlessly, stopping beside her. She nodded, her whole body trembling.

'Come on then' – taking her firmly by the arm – 'there's nothing we can do here now. Let's clear out before the other cats arrive.'

He began leading her back up the slope, but when they had gone only a short distance she tore free.

'It's best not to stay,' he told her gently. 'You know what's going to happen. There's no point in watching it.'

She lifted her head, her thick hair falling away from her cheeks and forehead. In the pale moonlight her features seemed to be brushed with silver, only her eyes sunk in shadow – the whole effect giving to her face the likeness of a stern, vengeful mask. 'Killers!' she muttered softly, showing no inclination to walk on.

'You can't blame them,' he answered, thinking that she was referring to the cats. 'It's their nature.'

'No, not the animals,' she corrected him. 'People like Molly!' She turned and pointed to where the lion was tearing at the lifeless body. 'Look!' she whispered fiercely, her voice cracking under the strain of feeling. 'D'you see that? A poor woman who didn't even ask to come in here! Who was dragged in against her will! And Molly makes that happen to her! For no reason!'

'Please, Ellie,' he begged, closing his eyes rather than look at what the lion was doing, 'let's just get away.'

He reached for her arm, but she again fended him off. Below them, a lioness crept from the bushes to join her mate.

'No, listen to me,' she insisted, 'it's important. If Molly can kill a poor defenceless woman for no reason, when there's not even any pressure on her, what will she do one day when she's threatened? Ask yourself that, Ben. What will she do then?'

121

'How should I know?' he said distractedly, not really trying to answer her question, concerned only with escaping the horror on the path below.

So that it was only later, lying in the stillness of his own room, the dim candlelight flickering uncertainly on the walls and ceiling, that the real meaning of her words came home to him.

CHAPTER TWELVE

What Ellie later referred to as the first threat against Molly occurred the following afternoon. In the upper corner of Taronga, high on the hillside, stood a tall artificial rock, originally constructed out of concrete for the benefit of such sure-footed animals as mountain goats and barbary sheep. Because of its height it had for some time been used as a lookout post. On that particular day a young woman was stationed up there, equipped with a rifle and a pair of binoculars. Early in the afternoon, during the quietest, most drowsy part of a warm day, a shot rang out and she toppled from her perch, her body rolling and bouncing down the steep rock-face.

Nobody realized what had happened to begin with. At the sound of the shot, Molly triggered the alarm and everyone adopted a defensive position; some people guarding the major buildings; others taking cover at specified points all over the park; Ellie and Ben running swiftly around the outer fence, searching for where a break-in might have taken place. It was only when someone was sent to the tall rock in order to check with the lookout that the body was found, lying crumpled on one of the lower ledges.

Molly was furious but also tight-lipped about the incident, giving no indication of what she intended doing.

'I suppose this means another night raid into Mosman,'

Ben said gloomily, confiding his fears to Ellie.

She shook her head. 'Not necessarily. This wasn't just revenge. I reckon it was also a warning.'

'A warning? Of what?'

'Someone's telling Molly that her raid didn't work. It's a way of showing her there're still armed people outside, who can hit back any time they please.'

'Chas,' Ben whispered involuntarily, recalling the brief glimpse he had been given of the horribly scarred face beneath the balaclava.

'Who?'

'It was probably Chas,' he explained, 'the leader of the gang that pushed me over the fence.'

'Could be.'

'So what can Molly do?' Ben wondered aloud.

Ellie shrugged. 'Nothing much. Just sit tight for a while.'

Which was precisely what happened. In the ensuing days there were frequent alarms. They always followed the same pattern: one or two random shots, which rarely found their mark now, fired by an unseen sniper from somewhere outside the boundary. Everyone would scuttle for cover, wondering if this was the beginning of the big attack, the tension increasing with each fresh disturbance. And yet still Molly did nothing, merely advising people to keep clear of the outer fence. Not until a week had gone by did she agree to discuss the problem openly, and only then because of the growing uncertainty within Taronga.

It was a short, stormy meeting, held as usual in the restaurant, with some people proposing a raid on the surrounding streets, and others insisting on defensive measures. Molly brought the discussion to an end, her face pale and scornful.

'Just look at you,' she said witheringly, gazing down at them from her vantage point on the chair, 'acting like animals in a cage. Getting all neurotic as soon as someone comes and peers at you through the bars. Don't you realize that those people out there want you to carry on like this? They know if they can rattle you enough, you'll be incapable of defending the place. Better still, you might be fool enough to go out there and try and take them on.'

'What's wrong with that?' someone asked. 'We could handle them.'

'What's wrong with it?' she repeated sarcastically. 'Can't you even work that out?'

There was a morose silence.

'All right,' she went on, 'then I'll tell you. Because a raiding party wouldn't find an enemy to fight. Sending people over the wire would only achieve one thing: it would weaken our defences in here. And that's when the big attack would come, when we were least prepared for it.'

The man called Terry, standing at the very edge of the crowd, called out, 'That's all very well, but what do we do in the meantime?'

'We wait,' Molly answered shortly.

'How long for?'

'For ever if necessary. And why not? After all, we're already holding what those people out there want. We don't *have* to do anything. They're the ones who'll be forced to act in the end. And when they do, when the fight comes, I want to make sure it's on our terms.' She clenched her fist and thrust it out towards them, much as they had once done to her. 'On our terms!' she repeated emphatically. 'Have you got that? Ours!' She paused, allowing her words to sink in. 'And afterwards . . . *then* we'll go over the wire if it's still necessary. That'll be the time to show them who's boss around here.'

There was no further debate after that, the crowd breaking up and wandering away in small groups. Alone with Ellie once more, Ben noticed how discouraged she looked.

'What did you make of that lot?' he asked.

They were walking along one of the upper paths and Ellie

stopped and stared at the city skyline, the tall buildings devoid now of purpose or meaning.

'It's war, isn't it?' she muttered unhappily. 'The same thing all over again. Two sides taking it in turns to fight in each other's territory.'

'And with our turn next,' he commented.

'Looks like it.'

A sudden disturbing thought occurred to Ben. 'But what about the animals? What'll happen to them if there's a battle in Taronga?'

Ellie surveyed the bush slope beneath them before raising her eyes once again to the stark city skyline. 'I don't know, Ben,' she said. 'That's something else we have to wait and find out about.'

It proved to be a long wait: three weeks crawling slowly by; the silence shattered at least once every day by unseen snipers. There were no further casualties now that everyone gave the outer fence a wide berth, but still those random shots achieved their purpose, for they increased the general feeling that Taronga was in a state of siege. In spite of Molly's warning, the air of uncertainty, of being constantly under threat, told steadily on everyone. Tempers became frayed, with arguments, and sometimes even fights, breaking out for no apparent reason. Even the animals began to sense that something was amiss. Instead of feeding peacefully, they would shy at the least noise or edge nervously away if someone approached.

Only Raja remained unaffected by the widespread uncertainty. Fearless by nature, he would roar out his usual challenge if anyone ventured near his cage; and at night he continued to haunt the lower reaches of Taronga where the low wall and the soft washing of the sea against the shore gave him a tantalizing sense of the freedom he yearned for. The only slight change in him was in his relationship to Ben. Ever since that night when they had briefly made contact, a tremor of understanding passing between them, he had been less defiant. More and more frequently, he began searching behind the word of command, feeling for the human mind which sheltered there. What he found made him snarl and draw back, but also puzzled and intrigued him. For in his primitive yet effective way, he could tell that Ben also felt caged, less free than he had formerly. And with that knowledge, those first glimmerings of fellow-feeling grew into something more. Not trust: that certainly didn't exist between them; given the opportunity, Raja would still have ended Ben's life with one swift slash of his paw. It was more a suggestion of shared sympathy, a passing recognition that they both had to deal with a common enemy.

A typical encounter occurred about a month after the first alarm. Ben had already released Ranee and was intent on enticing Raja from his cage. As the tiger stepped out into the darkening tunnel, he stopped and stared straight at Ben. They were no more than a metre apart; and at that precise moment, facing each other equally, it was impossible to say which of them was captive and which was free. For the space of a heartbeat – no more than that – they dropped their defences, each perceiving in the other's eyes an image of himself. Ben raised his hand, as if to reach out and touch the fiercely whiskered head, but the spell was already broken. And snarling half in bewilderment, half in resentment at this, the unexpected face of his enemy, Raja slid away along the tunnel and disappeared.

Ben walked more slowly to the opening. A fine rain was falling, the overcast sky making the evening feel more advanced than it really was. Already there were dark stains of shadow beneath the trees, and even in the open the atmosphere was tinged a dusky blue-grey. Looking out at the twilight, Ben was struck by the notion that an evening such as this was perfect for an assault on Taronga. The early dusk, the

127

poor visibility, the difficulty of following a scent in the rain – all pointed to a possible conflict. It was not a pleasant thought, but one which persuaded him to remain where he was for a while, all his senses on the alert.

The rain began to fall more heavily, dripping from the vine that swarmed around the tunnel opening; and a little more daylight ebbed away. Soon only the ghost of the day remained, a vague half-light that troubled his vision. As he screwed up his eyes, peering into the shadows, he knew that if he were in Chas's position this would be the moment he would choose. Now. And only seconds later, as though in response to his own unbidden fears, he heard the alarm. It was faint, far off, the sound only just reaching him, but unmistakable.

He needed no instructions. Leaping out into the rain, he followed the same course he had taken weeks earlier, making straight for the lower fence. He knew the exact spot he wanted: that section of wall where he had first been pitched into the darkness of Taronga. Now as then, it was the obvious place for Chas to attempt a break-in: the wall easy to scale; and Raja always somewhere in the vicinity, ready to pursue the unfortunate person pushed over as bait. Who would it be this time? And was the person inside yet or had they merely touched the alarm wires with the snips? Ben tried to recall the details of his own entry: the snipping of the wire; the hurried .conference; the brief delay as they waited for Raja to make his presence known. Yes, that had been the critical factor – Raja's whereabouts, his rumbling growl signalling to the waiting invaders.

Without slackening his pace, Ben opened his mind and searched the slope below. As he had hoped, Raja and Ranee were there, but still waiting; too distant for Ben to command, but perhaps close enough to be delayed. Using all his power, he sent out an urgent danger warning, and immediately felt them respond: Ranee flinching back, a thrill of fear passing through her; Raja hesitating slightly as he stopped and scented the breeze.

It was as much as Ben could have expected, Raja at least remaining silent while he searched for the source of danger. With luck, that might be all that was needed. Continuing to Call, Ben rapidly narrowed the distance between himself and the waiting tigers. Already he was on the lower path, running along it, plunging down into the thick bush bordering the wall.

He was brought to a skidding halt by Raja's growl, his feet almost shooting out from under him on the wet soil. That same growl, as he was sickeningly aware, would also act as a spur to the figures lurking on the other side of the wall. He listened, having to strain past the hammering of the rain on the leaves above him, and heard a familiar voice whisper hoarsely, 'That's it! Get him through!'

An equally familiar voice, shrill now with terror, replied, 'No, Chas! Please! I'll do anything! Anything!'

There was a brief scuffle, a sound of ripping cloth, and a soft thud as someone landed on the ground inside the wall.

'I can't!' the second voice wailed, 'I can't!'

'You touch that wall and I'll cut you!'

'No! The blood! If they smell blood . . . !'

'Then get going! Or else!'

The whispered argument continued in the background, but Ben was barely listening to it, his mind focussed on the tigers, willing them back. As always, Ranee responded at once, sidling away up the slope, only Raja pitting himself against Ben's unwelcome interference. Ordinarily, it was a contest Ben would have been reasonably confident of winning, but the argument between the figures at the wall suddenly ended in a cry of pain, and with a surge of energy Raja nearly broke free. It was clear what had happened: Chas had made good his threat and cut his victim, the smell of blood maddening Raja. He began roaring out in protest, tearing at the sodden undergrowth, and it required all Ben's strength and ability to hold him in check.

As he struggled to maintain control, there was another cry, this time of fear, and a thin figure scurried past him in the thickening darkness. Raja tried to follow and found his way blocked by Ben, the two of them face to face as they had been so often before. But now with this difference: the alluring scent of blood was like a bridge reaching out over the silent chasm of command, tempting Raja to cross it. He crept forward, the outline of his head only just distinguishable, and Ben, his scalp prickling with fear, was forced to give ground, his heels sliding treacherously on the wet bank.

'No!' he ordered, the rain streaming down his face. 'Keep back!'

To his astonishment, Raja stopped. Yet it wasn't Ben's spoken word of command which had halted his advance. Above the noise of Raja's roaring and the persistent drumming of the rain, Chas was heard to shout, 'Now the other one!'

And before Ben could even work out what those words might mean, Raja had turned and leaped for the wall, one paw striking out, silencing for ever the second of the intruders almost before his feet touched the ground.

Ben did not have to witness the death scene – the night and the rain together hid it from him. Yet Raja's contented growls told him plainly enough what had occurred, giving him a clear indication that there was nothing more he could do. As with Ranee and the prisoner . . .

The thought of Ranee suddenly alerted him to a new danger. She was still up there, wandering the hillside, and he had overlooked the threat she posed once before, with dire consequences.

Slipping and sliding on the muddy surface, he floundered his way up towards the path. What was it Chas had told him on that night when he too had been pushed over the wall?

The actual words came back to him: 'run diagonally across the hillside.' He followed exactly those instructions now – or as nearly as the cages and the meandering pathways would allow. And after a few minutes, much to his relief, he caught up with the thin figure that had pushed past him earlier.

The man's initial flight had taken him a considerable distance up the hillside; but in the rain-filled night he had lost his sense of direction and stopped. Now, overcome by terror, he was huddled at the side of the path, his spidery-thin legs drawn up against his body. He started hastily to his feet at the sight of Ben, his rat-like features thrust forward as he peered nervously through the darkness and rain. One cheek, Ben noticed, was cut open, a dark dribble of blood staining the stubbly line of his jaw.

'It's all right, Trev,' he said soothingly.

'What? Who's that?'

'You remember me? A couple of months back. You and Chas put me over the wall.'

He had meant to sound reassuring, but his words threw Trev into a renewed state of panic.

'That wasn't my idea!' he cried shrilly. 'I told him . . . !'

He stopped and stared wild-eyed past Ben to where Ranee had slid silently into view. She was only a short leap away, crouched low, her tail twitching.

'Bloody hell!' he burst out.

'I told you, it's all right,' Ben said in a steady voice. 'She won't attack while I'm here.'

He stepped towards Ranee and issued a sharp dismissive Call. She snarled, her eyes fixed hungrily on Trev; but after a brief hesitation she obediently loped off to join Raja.

'She's gone!' Trev whispered, clutching at Ben's sleeve. 'How the hell d'you manage that?'

'Never mind how. We'd better get you out of here while you're still alive.'

'Can you do it?' Both hands clutching even more desper-

131

ately at Ben's threadbare shirt. 'Can you get me back over the fence?'

'I think so. But only on one condition: you tell me the general plan of the attack.'

'I will! I promise. Once you get me to the fence.'

Ben shook his head, acting far more ruthless than he felt. 'No way. You give me the plan first.'

Trev glanced furtively behind him, his thin face pinched with anxiety, his lips slack and trembling. On every side the rain enclosed them like a fine grey-black curtain, rustling and murmuring as it brushed persistently against the grass and leaves of Taronga.

'It's your life you're risking, Trev,' Ben said.

But it was fear, not reluctance, which had made him hesitate. 'For God's sake!' he pleaded. 'I'll tell you anything, if only you'll . . . '

'The plan first,' he interrupted insistently.

Trev made a visible effort to steady himself, his small eyes screwed up in anguish. 'Okay, the plan.' He took a quick, gasping breath. 'There're four break-in points, all on the lower fence. The idea was to put decoys over first and then follow up with the others.'

'Others?'

'Armed men. About twenty of them.'

'And where're they making for?'

'The weatherboard house overlooking the harbour. That for starters. A base is what Chas called it.'

As if to support his account, there was a burst of automatic gunfire from down near the house, followed seconds later by a lingering scream. More shots and screams issued from the same area, all coming in quick succession. Trev, his meagre body shaking with fear, had again slumped into a helpless, crouching position, his head buried in his arms.

'Please,' he begged. 'They'll be here soon. The other cats!'

Ben, who had experienced similar moments of terror

within Taronga, urged him gently to his feet. He knew there was no time now to lead Trev to the fence, not with Ellie's life in danger. Yet he couldn't leave him out there in the open, defenceless. What he needed was a temporary place of sanctuary, somewhere close by.

'Come on,' he said, the perfect place suddenly occurring to him. 'I'm taking you where you'll be safe. But we have to move!'

Trev looked up, his thin features twisted into a mask of suspicion. 'You wouldn't trick me? Feed me to . . . them?'

The gunfire and the screams continued relentlessly in the background, Trev's face wincing at every sound.

'Don't be a fool!' Ben almost shouted, his concern for Ellie overriding his feelings of sympathy. 'If I wanted the cats to get you, all I'd have to do is leave you here. Now don't waste time.'

He turned away and began running towards the tiger cages situated a short distance across the hillside. Trev, anxious not to be left alone, followed close behind. He made no further protest until they reached the entrance to the tunnel. Then, as the pungent odour of big cat hit him full in the face, he drew back in alarm.

'It's a trick!' he shrilled out.

'The cats are gone,' Ben explained quickly. 'This is the safest place in Taronga until dawn.'

Taking Trev firmly by the arm, he drew him through the opening and into the first of the cages. The interior was so dark that Trev didn't realize he was being locked up until Ben lowered the cage door and secured it with a padlock.

'What are you up to?' he shouted hysterically. 'You can't leave me! Not here in the dark!'

But Ben had already pocketed the key. 'I'll be back before sunrise,' he said. 'I promise.'

Ignoring Trev's agonized pleas, he ran off through the steadily falling rain, heading straight for the weatherboard house on the far side of the park.

The firing had ceased by the time he reached it. An uneasy silence hung over that whole corner of Taronga, the house in darkness, the surrounding undergrowth strangely restless and alive. Ben, crouched in the long grass bordering the pathway, opened his mind and listened – and immediately detected the presence of a number of cats. They were in a state of nervous excitement, made wary by the recent gunfire, but also attracted by it, associating it, as always, with the prospect of food. Much of that 'food', Ben realized with a shudder, was already lying in the undergrowth all about him. Over to his left, there was a low-pitched growling as several cats worried at a dead body. Further along the path and directly in his line of vision, a full-maned lion stole stealthily towards the cover of nearby trees, dragging a recognizably human shape between its front legs.

Even for Ben it was a dangerous place, the cats raised to a pitch of excitement that made them unpredictable. Yet he knew that if Ellie were alive, there was a good chance she would still be somewhere in the vicinity. She would not have run off until she had checked whether there were any wounded people requiring help. He was sure of that.

Raising his head above the level of the grass, he called in a loud whisper, 'Ellie? Ellie, are you there?'

A short distance from where he crouched, something moved in the wet grass, making a faint swishing sound. Thinking it was one of the cats, he sent out a frantic danger signal. But the movement was followed by nothing more terrifying than a groan; and when he investigated, crawling forward on hands and knees, he came upon the woman called Val. She was lying curled up on her side, her eyes closed, both hands still clutching a rifle. One of her trouser legs was black with fresh blood.

Ben leaned over and touched her cheek lightly with his fingertips. 'Val,' he whispered, 'can you hear me?'

Her eyelids fluttered open, her eyes focussing on the outline of something hovering above her. With a scream of fear, she brought the rifle swinging round, her finger groping for the trigger. Ben tried to draw back, but the barrel struck him on the cheek, simultaneously discharging a gush of automatic fire. The noise alone rendered him almost senseless, deafening him in one ear; and the closeness of the discharge left him with burns down the whole side of his face.

Clutching at his head, blind with pain and shock, he reeled away, lurching uncertainly to his feet. In the few brief seconds before he fell, the night seemed to close relentlessly upon him: the rain like fire upon the seared skin of his face; his ears filled with a muffled roaring which, in his confusion, he could not distinguish from the challenge of lion or leopard. He tried to Call, to protect himself, but failed, his mind too numb to respond. Reaching out through the darkness, he touched something live and warm: the hard, compact feel of muscle and bone straining to reach him. There was no resisting it – he lacked both the purpose and the energy. And with a short sobbing breath, he submitted. As he toppled backwards, his last distinct thought was not of his own imminent death, but of Raja's fiercely beautiful face. 'If only ... if only ... ' he muttered audibly, his voice, sick with longing and regret, trailing away into emptiness.

CHAPTER THIRTEEN

He couldn't see the fire, but he could feel it, the hot yellow tips of flame scorching his hair and skin, making him jerk his head sideways. The pain persisted, a sharp burning sensation that originated somewhere within himself, erupting through the passive flesh of his face. It remained constant even when he opened his eyes and stared up at the shadowy outline of trees, felt the stinging raindrops on his throbbing cheek and temple. One of the trees seemed to move, swinging down towards him, feathery tufts of leaves brushing soothingly against his skin.

'Ben?' a voice said anxiously. 'Ben?'

He stirred, half sitting up, and found that Ellie was leaning over him, her thick hair hanging down in wet strings, her face streaming with rain. She was breathing heavily, as if from recent exertion.

'Can you hear me?' she said.

Her voice sounded blurred and distant, as though one of his ears were blocked. He reached up to touch it, his fingers encountering instead the badly burned skin on the side of his face. Everything came back to him then – the alarm, the gunfire, the aura of carnage all around the house.

'Where are the cats?' he cried, clambering shakily to his feet.

She encircled his shoulders with both arms, steadying him until he regained his balance. 'They're back there,' she said. 'I dragged you clear.'

'And Val?'

She shrugged helplessly. 'I had to choose between you. I couldn't get you both away.'

'But there're people in the house,' he protested. 'Why didn't you call for help?'

'The attack was successful,' she explained quietly. 'They've taken the house. They fire on anyone who goes near.'

'So Val . . . ?'

She nodded. 'It was one of the leopards mainly: I couldn't keep him off. And Val had a bad wound. The smell of blood . . . there was nothing I could do.'

He could hear them now, through the murmur of rain: the growls and fierce snuffling of big cats feeding.

'This is the start of it then,' he said miserably. 'A war right here in Taronga.'

'It may not be as bad as that,' she answered more hopefully. 'Molly's not the kind of person to let something like this go on for long.'

'I don't see what she can do to stop it. There are two rival groups in here now. Give them time and they'll turn this hillside into a battlefield.'

'I wouldn't underestimate Molly . . .' she began.

But their voices had disturbed some of the cats. A lioness, feeling that her kill was threatened, gave a warning snarl and came charging towards them through the darkness. Ellie sprang for the nearest tree, swarming up between the rain-soaked branches; but Ben remained where he was, sending out a warning Call. It was too late to halt the charge, yet sufficient to make the lioness veer around him and go crashing off through the undergrowth. Still holding her at a safe distance, he sent her, growling with resentment, back to her kill.

Ellie dropped down beside him. 'Time to clear out,' she

137

murmured. 'Can you make it all right?'

'I think so.'

Moving slowly, they crossed the park to the restaurant. Steve unlocked the door.

'Where the hell have you two been?' he said angrily, dragging them inside.

The main room was like the interior of a fortress, with guns and boxes of ammunition laid out on the floor in readiness. Some of the boxes, larger than the rest and painted a dull khaki, had been stacked in one corner. Molly, as usual, was stationed by the phone, surrounded by a group of young men and women, all of them dressed in jungle greens, with ammunition-and grenade-belts around their waists.

'Well?' she asked sharply.

'They've taken the house,' Ellie said.

'I thought so. What happened to the people inside?'

'I think they're dead.'

Molly showed no surprise, no disappointment, merely glancing at Ben's damaged face. 'Get that seen to while you have the chance,' she said. 'We may need everyone we've got later on.'

One of the young women took him through to the kitchen where she smeared whitish ointment on his burn. Just touching the wound made it smart painfully, but afterwards it felt a little better, the stinging pain subsiding to a dull ache.

When he returned to the main room, Molly was still asking Ellie about the attack.

'So the ones the cats didn't get are all inside the house?'

'Yes.'

'How d'you know that? Couldn't there be more somewhere else? Hiding in the animal cages, for instance?'

'No, Ellie's right,' Ben interrupted. 'They were only interested in taking the house.'

Molly swung round to face him. 'What makes you so sure?'

'I questioned one of them. He told me the plan was to set

138

up a base there.'

Molly's eyes narrowed. 'And where is this informant now?'

Ben barely hesitated. 'I let Raja have him, down near the wall.'

'Is that where your face got burned?'

'No, that happened over by the house, when we were trying to save some of the wounded.'

Molly sighed impatiently. 'I'm glad to hear you at least tried. That's better than nothing. Though from now on I'm looking for results.' She glanced questioningly at Steve who was standing just beyond the ring of listeners. 'Could you ferret that rabble out of the house using light weaponry?'

He made a dubious gesture with both hands. 'It'd be risky. They'd be the ones fighting from cover, and we'd have the cats to contend with.'

'Well I'm not leaving them holed up in there!' she snapped back irritably. 'There'll be nothing to stop them bringing reinforcements in once the cats crawl off for a sleep. Then where will we be? Before we know what's happening, we'll be looking down the barrel of the Doomsday plan. That's all we'll have left.'

The word Doomsday sounded an oddly hollow note in the silence of the room, carrying with it an icy breath of chaos.

'Doomsday?' Ben asked. 'What's that?'

Only Ellie heard him, all the rest of them too absorbed in their immediate problems to pay him any attention.

'There's one sure way of getting them out,' Steve said and jerked his thumb towards the boxes stacked in the corner, 'but it'll cost you the house.'

Molly eyed the boxes. 'I'm not too worried about the house,' she answered, 'just as long as we clear Taronga before dawn. Could you hit them with that thing?'

Steve grinned, unconsciously flexing his shoulder muscles. 'There'd be a bit of trial and error till we got the range. After that – boom! No more trouble.'

'All right,' Molly said, 'set it up outside, next to the rotunda. You should be able to get a sighting from there. Use flares if you have to. Ben and Ellie will keep the area clear of cats.'

There was an eager scramble to unpack the boxes. Ben, watching the khaki-coloured metal parts being taken out and fitted together, didn't at first recognize the thing being constructed. But when the final box was opened and the long swollen-bodied projectiles lifted out, he understood.

'Those are mortars!' he said to Molly in a shocked voice.

'And so?'

'There are cats down there, all round the house! You could kill them!'

'We can spare a few cats,' Molly answered casually. 'We can spare anything if we have to.'

'At least let me try and clear them from the danger zone,' he pleaded.

She dismissed the idea. 'Not a chance. If we take the pressure off the house, that scum could break out and start swarming all over Taronga. I'm not endangering what we've got here for a few cats.'

'But Taronga belongs to them too!' he burst out – and realized his error as he saw the closed expression on Molly's face. 'Maybe you're right,' he conceded, feigning a humility he didn't feel. 'It's the people in here that matter. Us. Though there could be a better way of clearing the house. What if I went down there and talked to them? Told them you were going to start lobbing mortars? That might scare them off. And you wouldn't have to wreck the building.'

'How long do we stick around here chatting?' Steve broke in. He was standing in the middle of the room, hefting one of the mortar shells from hand to hand, a smile of anticipation on his face.

'No, wait a minute,' Molly said thoughtfully. 'Ben might have something It would be worthwhile saving the house.

We could double the guard and cut off any attack there in the future. Without it, we're wide open in that part of the park – unless we start converting cages into a guard post. And we could do without that kind of hassle right now.'

'Suit yourself,' Steve answered, unable to hide his disappointment.

Molly mused silently before raising her clear green eyes towards Ben. 'I seem to remember giving you half an hour once before,' she said evenly. 'Well I'm giving you the same amount of time now. After that, Steve gets a free hand.'

'That's not long,' he objected. 'I'll have to talk to them, persuade them. Couldn't you make it an hour?'

'You heard me. Thirty minutes. Then time's up.'

He knew Molly well enough not to argue. Nodding his agreement, he hurried to the door. Ellie, anticipating Molly's decision, was already waiting there.

'No, not you,' he said gently.

'Why not?'

'You know what it's like near the house.'

'All the more reason to give you a hand.'

He looked at her face: so open, so . . . he hunted for the right word: yes, that was it, honest; so much younger and more innocent than he himself felt, even though their ages were almost identical.

'I'd like you to come,' he told her. 'Really. But if anything happens – well, there'll still be one of us left.'

Her eyes seemed to cloud over for a moment. 'I wouldn't want to stay here if anything like that happened,' she answered quietly.

'You'd have to, Ellie. Who else would look after the cats?' He knew she would have no answer to that.

'Be careful then,' she murmured, opening the door for him, brushing his hand with hers as he stepped outside.

Seconds later he was again following the winding paths, running swiftly to the far side of Taronga. The rain continued to fall, though it had slackened to a fine drizzle that drifted lazily out of the blackness, caressing his damaged face with the lightness and delicacy of mist. After the closed-up atmosphere of the restaurant, the night was refreshingly cool, and by the time he reached the house he felt calm and clear-headed, with a little of the hearing returning to his deafened ear.

Despite the pressure of time, he approached the house not from the front, where the broad pathway gave him no cover, but from the upper side – creeping through the overgrown garden to within sight of a smashed and splintered window. There was no light inside, no sign of life. The only sound, which even his defective hearing could detect, was of feeding cats. Several of them had growled restlessly at his approach, but had soon settled down as they recognized his familiar scent.

Taking cover behind a large tree, he called loudly, 'Chas, are you in there?'

The answer was a rapid succession of shots that ripped through the leaves above his head. As he ducked down, a chorus of roars and growls greeted the noise.

'Listen to me,' he shouted. 'That won't achieve anything. All you'll do is upset the cats and make it more difficult for me to get you safely out of there.'

He tried to emphasize the word 'safely', hoping it would arouse their curiosity, but now only silence greeted his words.

'Chas?' he called again. 'Can you hear me?'

This time there was a suggestion of movement just inside the window, and a hoarse voice, which he remembered only too well, answered him. 'What do you want?'

'I have a proposition for you.'

'What kind of proposition?'

'Safe conduct over the fence, for you and your men, if you agree to clear out now.'

A humourless rumble of laughter issued from the darkness.

'You call that a proposition? What's in it for us?'

'Your lives. If you stay, they're going to blast you out with mortars. You haven't got much time to decide.'

'You're bluffing,' Chas shouted back.

'It's the truth, I swear it. They're training the mortars on this area now. They'll blow it to smithereens if you stick around. I can get you out if you want. What do you say?'

There was furtive whispering inside the house. He waited expectantly, but as the minutes ticked by he began to lose heart. Why should they accept his proposition, he asked himself hopelessly. They had paid dearly for the capture of the house: they weren't likely to give it up without a fight.

All at once he felt tired and unwell. His face hurt unbearably and there was a painful tingling sensation in his ear as his hearing gradually improved. Leaning back against the tree, he was about to slump to the ground when he was startled by Chas again calling to him.

'If we agree to leave, how'll you get us past the cats?'

All Ben's feelings of tiredness and despair left him at once. 'You'll go then?'

'Only if you can guarantee to keep those animals off our backs.'

'No problem. I'm the one who controls them. As long as you stay close to me you'll be fine.'

The same mirthless laughter floated from the window. 'D'you think we were born yesterday?' A metallic click, of someone loading a gun, accompanied the voice.

'Hold on!' Ben said hastily. 'Just work it out. Someone has to control them, and if I'm not the one, then how come I'm standing out here now? Why aren't the cats attacking me?'

Again there was a whispered discussion, but much briefer this time. 'Fair enough,' Chas said at last. 'But you make the first move, and be sure it's not your last. Drop any arms you're carrying and walk slowly down the path in front of the house so we can have a look at you.'

Ben's stomach lurched unpleasantly. He had known that this moment would have to come, yet still the prospect of walking out into the open made him quail inside.

'Give me a minute to reach the path,' he said in an unsteady voice.

But it was only a delaying tactic, a brief space in which to gather his failing courage. With a trembling hand, he wiped the rain and sweat from his forehead. Then, taking a deep breath, he pushed his way through the bushes towards the path.

That first step into the open was the most testing part. For several seconds he couldn't move, standing quite still at the edge of the path, his stomach muscles aching with tension. Strangely, it was Chas who reassured him.

'We're waiting,' he called out.

'Yes . . . yes, I'm coming.'

Much calmer now, he Called to any cats, warning them away, and walked slowly down past the front of the house. The side door opened a fraction and a torchlight shone out, dazzling him.

'D'you see who it is, Chas?' a voice said excitedly. 'It's that kid we put through the wire months ago.'

The torch was clicked off.

'So he was from in here after all,' Chas murmured, the words only just reaching Ben.

'No, I wasn't,' Ben answered quickly, eager to avoid any misunderstanding while he was standing undefended on the path. 'I proved I could handle the animals – that's why they let me stay. That's also why they sent me down here tonight.'

'Okay, we get the message,' Chas said. 'We're coming out. But I'm warning you, any sign of a sniper and you're dead.'

The door opened wider and a group of shadowy figures emerged, pausing in the partial cover of the side wall before sidling out onto the path. Even in the near darkness Ben could see why they had accepted his proposition. Of the original twenty, only five had survived; and three of them were obviously wounded, barely able to drag themselves along.

'Is this all?' Ben asked.

Chas, himself unwounded, crept up beside Ben, his balaclava transforming his head into a formless blob of darkness. 'Expensive hobby, this Taronga business,' he answered. With a chuckle, he raised his rifle and tapped Ben lightly on the side of the face, making him gasp with pain. 'I see you didn't get off scot-free either,' he added, and chuckled again. 'What're you trying to do, qualify for a job with me?'

One of the other men laughed aloud, as though sharing some private joke with his leader.

'Better not talk too much,' Ben cautioned them. 'It'll rouse the cats.'

In total silence, stopping occasionally so the wounded could rest, Ben led them the short distance to the lower fence. For most of the brief journey he encountered no problems, the cats around the house too wary of his warning signals to leave their kills. But just as they reached the fence he became uneasily aware of Raja's presence somewhere on the slope above them. Having eaten his fill, he was no longer hungry, yet Ben could sense that there was still a dangerous alertness about him.

'We've got to be quick,' he whispered. 'There're tigers around. They're the hardest to handle.'

He felt Chas stiffen beside him, and his voice, when he replied, was more hoarse than usual. 'We cut the wire just along here.'

Half dragging the wounded between them, they soon reached the hole: a space big enough for a man to slide through, but too small for any of the predators. Chas ducked through first, followed more slowly by the wounded. Ben, preoccupied with helping them escape, momentarily forgot

145

about Raja. Bending down, he again pulled back the jagged ends of wire.

'Now you,' he said to the last man – and at that moment felt his arms pinioned from behind.

'Got him, Chas!' the man shouted, and laughed.

'Good on you. Push him through to me.'

Ben felt himself being forced downwards, closer to the hole. 'But we had an agreement!' he protested, too surprised even to struggle.

'What d'you take me for?' Chas answered. 'A mug? With you to keep the cats off, we can walk into this place next time.'

Ben's head and shoulders were already through the opening, a piece of wire snagging in the thin material of his shirt. Only then did he start to struggle. 'No!' he cried, jerking backwards, squirming and kicking in an attempt to break the grip on his arms.

'You'll have to give me a hand, Chas!' the man gasped, grunting with the effort of holding on to him. He swung Ben around, the two of them crashing into the wire. 'Where the hell's that hole?' he said angrily.

'Over to your right.'

Chas clicked on the torch, to help his companion. But the beam, in revealing the position of the opening, shone through the fence onto the bush-covered hillside. To Chas, concerned mainly with the struggle taking place, that living backdrop consisted of nothing more than tufted grass and glistening foliage. Only Ben, used to the camouflage effect of a tiger's striped coat, saw something else: Raja's face peering out at him; the eyes, caught in the torchlight, like silver-black hollows.

With a shock of recognition he stopped struggling, his mind probing outwards. But everything was too tangled, too many things happening at once for him to exert adequate control. The torchbeam swung away from the opening and onto his own face, shining full on the charred and blistered

146

skin, revealing his wound to the crouching tiger. And almost simultaneously Raja's mind reached out and touched his own – a shock of recognition there too, Raja's response so unexpected, so unlike anything he had experienced before, that he gave way before it, allowing the savage animal intelligence to surge through him.

For a moment he lost all sense of his own identity. It was as if he were thinking Raja's thoughts, seeing through Raja's eyes, gathering and tightening those powerful muscles which were about to launch . . . Ben could not face what must follow. With a faint whimper of dread, he closed his mind, severing the link that bound them, just as Raja roared and burst from cover. Cowering down, his arms still pinioned behind him, he felt the cool wind of the heavy paw as it passed above his head and thudded into receptive flesh. Then the sheer weight of the charge sent him rolling over and over in the sodden grass, his arms and legs entwined in the dead limbs of the man who had been holding him.

Before he could rise, there was an eruption of automatic fire from the other side of the fence.

'That bastard animal!' Chas screamed out, playing the torch over the now empty section of hillside. 'I'll kill it! I swear I'll bloody kill it! If it's the last thing I do!'

Ben disentangled himself from the dead body and crawled into the cover of the bush. For a while longer the light continued to sweep over the hillside. He waited for it to go out and then crept slowly away. He had not gone far when Chas called to him.

'Hey, Kid!' His voice was less distorted now by hatred, but no less determined. 'Take a message for me. Tell that Molly character I'm not finished yet. I'm going to take this place even if I have to tear it apart in the process. You tell her that.'

PART III

THE ANSWER

CHAPTER FOURTEEN

Ben slipped back into the restaurant just as Steve was preparing to take the mortar cannon outside.

'There's no need for that now,' he said. 'The house is empty. I led them down to the fence myself.'

'So they've all gone?' Molly asked, the relief showing on her face, the hard lines between her mouth and nose softening slightly.

'There were only five left,' Ben explained. 'And Raja got one of them as they were going back through the wire.'

Molly burst into throaty laughter. 'D'you hear that, Steve? The boy's learning at last.' She came across the room and put her arm around Ben's shoulder. 'That was well done,' she said admiringly. 'A really good job.'

It was the first time she had ever praised him. Under other circumstances it would have made him feel uncomfortable; but after the events of the night he was too drained to care.

'Yeah, thanks,' he muttered vaguely and made for the stairs. Just before he reached them, he remembered something else he had meant to tell her. 'Oh, the leader of the gang that broke in – a bloke called Chas – he asked me to pass on a message.'

'What kind of message?'

'He said he wasn't finished yet. That he'd take Taronga

151

even if he had to tear it apart.'

Molly raised her eyebrows in mock surprise. 'What am I supposed to do, tremble in my shoes?'

'I thought you'd better know, that's all.'

She smiled expansively. 'Well, when you're next in a position to take one of his messages,' she said wryly, 'you can tell him this from me: that if there's ever a question of this place being torn apart, we'll be the ones to do it.'

Ben frowned. 'What d'you mean?' – though already he was filled with a sense of foreboding.

'What I say,' Molly answered shortly. 'Taronga's ours. It'll never belong to anyone else. Steve and I decided that long ago. Anyone who kicks us out will soon find there's nothing left to take over.'

An earlier conversation came back to Ben. 'Is that what you meant by the Doomsday plan?'

She nodded. 'Don't let it worry you though. It'd only be a last resort.'

'You mean you'd kill all the animals?' His voice was oddly quiet, controlled.

'What else do you expect us to do? Hand them over with our blessing?'

'But to kill them? I don't see the point.'

'The point lies in the threat,' she explained, less friendly now, sensing his disapproval. 'Like any threat, it's a weapon, that we'd be foolish not to use. Just think about it – destroy us and you destroy Taronga. Doomsday. Even a child can understand that. It's what people used to call the ultimate deterrent. A last line of defence.'

'But that's like Last Days!' he burst out.

'What did you say?' Her face became suddenly red with indignation; the words themselves so heavy with anger that they stilled every other sound in the room.

'I'm sorry,' Ben mumbled, aware that it was pointless arguing with her. 'I'm tired, that's all.' And he turned and stumbled upstairs to his room.

Ellie joined him soon afterwards. 'Shall I light a candle?' she asked.

'No, not yet.'

He groped his way to the window and took down the shutter. The rain had stopped, the cloud cover slowly breaking up, small pockets of stars starting to appear. By their faint light he could make out the silhouette of the distant city, the gaunt buildings like giant tombstones planted along the horizon.

'You knew about the Doomsday plan, didn't you?' he said quietly.

Ellie was crouched near the door, her skin blending into the darkness, only her eyes visible.

'I didn't actually know about it,' she answered, 'but I guessed. I've been here long enough to work out people like Molly. And Dad warned me about them anyway, while I was still living outside.'

'What did he say?'

'That people who don't have much of a past probably don't have much of a future either.'

'Not much of a future,' Ben muttered, leaning against the window, his breath misting the pane and obscuring the dim outline of the city. He turned back towards the warm darkness of the room. 'What're we going to do, Ellie?' he said helplessly.

'What we're doing now. Keep things going as long as we can. For the animals' sake.'

'But in the end?'

'You never know, when the time comes we might be able to save some of them.'

'And we might not. Which'll make us as guilty as Molly. All we'll have done is keep them caged up until she's ready to shoot them!'

'They'll have been alive in the meantime,' Ellie objected.

153

'That's something.'

'They deserve more than that!' he said, his frustration erupting into anger. 'If we had any guts we'd smash down the fences.'

'How can we? We wouldn't stand a chance against the rest of them.'

'Why should they even know . . . know . . . ?'

He stopped and rubbed his hand hastily across the window pane, clearing it. Ellie, sensing a change in him, padded silently across the room and peered over his shoulder.

'What is it?' she asked, thinking he had seen something outside.

He said nothing for a minute or two; and when he did answer, his question seemed unconnected to their previous conversation. 'Taronga,' he said thoughtfully, 'the word itself, what did you say it means?'

'Water views.'

'Views . . . ' He mulled silently over the word.

'Why d'you ask?'

'Water views,' he repeated in the same thoughtful tone. 'That's pretty vague, isn't it?'

'I suppose so.'

'Taronga, as a word, could describe a thousand different places in Australia,' he went on with gathering enthusiasm. 'No, wait a minute – it could describe Australia itself. A country surrounded by water, looking out onto the oceans.'

'I don't see what you're getting at.'

'Yes, that's it!' he said excitedly. 'The whole of Australia. They can't destroy that, can they? Only each other. And that's something they'd do anyway. Except that we'll be choosing the time. And the place! Their place, not ours any more. Theirs!'

Ellie took him by the shoulders and swung him round. His face was more animated than she had ever seen it.

'What are you talking about?' she asked.

154

'About their war,' he answered. 'We'll let them have it. We'll even help . . . '

All at once another thought occurred to him: something he should have remembered earlier, but which now fitted perfectly with his new frame of mind. Releasing the lock on the window, he opened it as wide as it would go, allowing the damp earth smell and the fainter odour of the sea to sweep into the room.

'What are you doing?' she asked.

He was already climbing outside, edging down the tiled roof. 'I won't be long,' he whispered. 'I'll explain everything when I get back.'

He swung himself over the edge and dropped lightly to the ground. The sky was almost clear now, with just enough starlight to guide him easily to the tiger cages.

Trev was still inside, moaning softly to himself in the darkness. 'Who's that?' he asked in a frightened voice.

'It's only me, Ben.'

'Thank God! It's been terrible in here on my own.'

Ben selected a key on the ring hanging from his belt. He could just see Trev's pale face between the bars.

'The break-in was a failure,' he explained, 'but I still think I can get you out of here. If I do, will you take a message to Chas for me?'

'I'll do anything, I swear it!' he promised fervently, clutching at the bars.

'Right, here's the message. If he wants Taronga, he can have it. I'll give it to him on a plate.'

'*You* will?'

'Yes. I'll fix it so he can walk straight through the place.'

'How'll you manage it?'

'That's something I'll explain to Chas in person. Ask him to meet me down by the lower fence tomorrow night.'

Trev's pale face drew back slightly. 'He'd never buy that

idea. Not Chas. He'd think you were up to something. Setting a trap maybe.'

Ben thought quickly. 'I'll meet him outside then. On his own ground. Any place he chooses.'

'Yeah, he'd probably agree to that.'

'Okay. Tell him to decide on a place and send a guide for me. That way he can't be trapped. I'll meet the guide down by the wharf tomorrow night, as soon after dark as I can make it.'

Unlocking the padlock, he pulled it free and raised the door. Trev scurried out and stood nervously beside him in the gloom of the tunnel.

'What happens now?' he asked.

'Just stay a pace or two behind me,' Ben warned him. 'And don't make any noise.'

He stepped warily through the wide opening and probed the night for signs of predators, but after all the activity Taronga had settled into a period of calm.

'Come on,' Ben muttered, and set off at a run, making for the same hole in the fence that Chas had used.

In the course of their journey they were challenged several times, cats growling at them from the undergrowth bordering the path; but Ben Called reassuringly and they were allowed past, reaching the fence without mishap.

'This is the spot,' Ben said, holding back the severed ends of wire while Trev squirmed through.

Once on the other side, a little of Trev's old insolence returned. 'So why d'you want to help Chas all of a sudden?' he asked suspiciously. 'He's hardly your best mate. Not after putting you over the fence like that.'

Ben was prepared for such a question. 'Chas'll be doing me a favour,' he said, trying to sound bitter and spiteful. 'He'll be getting back at that lot for me.' He jerked his thumb towards the restaurant.

'Why, what'd they do to you? You're in with them, aren't you?'

'I was. Not any more. Not after this!' He turned his head and pointed to his damaged cheek.

Trev brought his face close to the wire, squinting in the faint starlight. 'Looks pretty bad.'

'It feels pretty bad too!' Ben said belligerently. 'And they're not getting away with it. They're going to pay!'

Trev let out a short unpleasant laugh. 'Yeah, Chas'll understand that. Especially as it's your face they had a go at.'

'So you'll tell him?'

'No worries.'

And with a quick stealthy movement he slid away into the darkness, leaving Ben alone in the cool, clear night.

He began walking back across the hillside, but after only a short distance he stopped and looked up. The great dome of the sky, black, star-sprinkled, arched above him, appearing at that moment so limitless, so vast and free, that the fences and cages of Taronga were dwarfed, reduced to the point where they barely seemed to exist – this hillside, and the huge continent stretching on and on beyond it, all part of that untrammelled space which had endured since the beginning of time.

The sun had set, the dusk thickening into night, when Ellie ran along the path to meet him.

'Mine are all out,' she said.

'Mine too.'

'So what have you decided? I can turn the power off if you like, but I don't fancy your chances of getting over the fence without a ladder. And we can't smuggle one of those out of the store. It's the overhanging part of the fence, the bit Steve added, that's the problem. You could cut yourself to pieces on the coils of barbed wire. Also, it'd be risky switching the power off while everyone's up and about.'

Ben nodded reluctantly. 'It'd be safer to go on with the digging. I just hope Chas doesn't give up on me.'

'He'll wait if he's really interested,' she reassured him.

In the fading light they headed for a stretch of fence close to the tiger cages. It was very tall at this point, made of closely woven steel mesh covered in a smother of ivy, the whole structure screened from the rest of Taronga by a cluster of trees and bushes.

Ben stooped at the base of the fence and dragged away a leafy branch, revealing a hole in the ground. It was already a good size, the result of his working at it on and off throughout the day – something which had not been particularly difficult with so many people mending the fence or burying the remains of dead bodies further down the hillside. Now he groped in the nearby bushes and pulled out a pick and shovel. Taking it in turns to dig, they began deepening the hole. The most difficult part was burrowing under the mesh without touching the lowest trip wire. On hands and knees, Ben jabbed carefully with the pick, while Ellie scraped the loose soil away with her bare hands.

'It strikes me,' Ben said, pausing for a moment to rest, 'that one of these days someone's going to use this method to get in.'

'They've already tried it on,' Ellie answered, 'some time back.'

'And what happened?'

'Not much. The noise of the digging attracted most of the cats. Before the hole was half finished they were so excited they must have leaped at the wire, because all the buzzers sounded. No one ever tried it again.'

'I'm not surprised,' Ben said ruefully, wiping sweat from his face and grinning at Ellie.

But a few minutes later the task was complete: a narrow trench scooped out under the wire.

'Here goes,' Ben muttered and squirmed along it, his back passing just beneath the lower strands of mesh. Once on the other side he was hidden from Ellie by the ivy.

'How does it feel to be free?' she whispered.

'Scary,' he answered truthfully, looking about him at the shadowy outline of the bush. After the enclosed, known spaces of Taronga, it appeared strange and threatening. 'Well, I'll see you in an hour or two,' he said, trying to sound casual.

'Take care.'

He picked his way through the bush to the road that half-encircled Taronga. It sloped downhill like a smooth black ribbon, flanked on one side by the Zoo and on the other by the National Park that extended out onto the headland. He began running, following the road round past the closed-up exit building towards the wharf. They were lying in wait for him there: four dark figures, one of them tall and thin, skulking in the deep shadow of the cliff.

'We nearly gave you away,' Trev said.

'It's harder getting out of that place than getting in,' Ben answered.

'Yeah, I guessed that might be the trouble. Anyway, we'd better move. Chas doesn't like being kept waiting.'

They led him back over the route he had once followed with Chas – along a narrow path which wound through the strip of thick bush bordering the harbour; a path which ended in the park facing onto the beach where Trev had captured him. From there, they took him not to their former hideout, but to a burned-out ruin several streets away. A large double garage, at the back of the property, was still intact, and Chas was waiting for him there. As usual he was wearing the balaclava, only his small close-set eyes visible in the flickering candlelight.

'So what's this plan of yours?' he asked, coming straight to the point. He sounded neither doubtful nor enthusiastic – merely neutral, as though what Ben might have to say hardly concerned him.

'It's like I told Trev,' Ben answered, 'I can give you Taronga if you want it.'

'Details are all I want right now.' His speech was clipped, non-committal.

159

Ben squatted on the earth floor and drew a rough outline of Taronga. 'Your big mistake,' he explained, 'has been trying to get in at the bottom of the hill. I know the fence isn't high there, but it's too far from the nerve-centre.' He jabbed a finger at the map, much higher up the hillside, close to the boundary fence and the road. 'This is where Molly hangs out, in the old restaurant. That's what you've got to take. If you can get hold of it, the rest'll be easy.'

Chas, unable to sustain his pretended indifference any longer, picked up a candle and crouched beside him. 'I know that bit of the fence,' he said hoarsely. 'You'd need a tank to get through it in a hurry. Before we could cut a hole or burrow under it, they'd blast us to kingdom come.'

'Not if it was partly cut beforehand,' Ben said quietly.

'That'd help,' Chas conceded.

'And not if the alarm was turned off. You could hit the restaurant before they knew what was happening.'

Chas looked at him, his eyes gleaming greedily. 'Could you work that? Turn off the power?'

Ben nodded. 'The switch is right here behind the restaurant.' He again pointed at the crude outline in the dust.

Chas leaned forward, his sour breath making Ben edge away. 'That still leaves the cats. What about them?'

'There won't be any cats. I won't let them out.'

'Doesn't anybody check up on you?'

'There's an Aboriginal girl who helps handle them, but I can fix her. She won't be any problem.'

Chas stood up and paced thoughtfully off into the shadows. At the far end of the garage he turned and faced back to where Ben was still crouched in the candlelight.

'And you're prepared to help us,' he said evenly, 'just to get your own back on this Molly character.'

'I don't see it like that,' Ben replied. 'As far as I'm concerned, it'll be you who's helping me.'

Chas didn't move, his muscular body like a darker area of shadow against the far wall. 'Trev never mentioned what they did to you,' he said, speaking in slow measured terms.

It was this part of the meeting that Ben had prepared for most carefully and he immediately leaped up, as though stirred to anger by the memory of the previous evening.

'It was last night,' he explained in a strained voice, 'when they told me to go down and talk to you. I refused at first because it sounded risky. They didn't argue or anything. Steve – that's Molly's right-hand man – he just picks up a lighted pressure lamp and bashes me with it. Molly didn't try and stop him, even though she must have known it'd do something like this.'

Chas's hand, in involuntary sympathy, jerked up towards his masked face. Yet he still didn't come any nearer: standing there half-hidden in the gloom. 'That's not the kind of thing you forgive,' he said. 'You'd have to be a saint to let it go.'

'Well I'm no saint!' Ben broke out vehemently. And then, as if inviting the next question, 'A second after that lamp hit me, I knew I was going to get them, no matter what it cost.'

Chas's response came just a little too quickly. 'Yeah, though that's been puzzling me a bit. Why didn't you make this offer to me last night?'

'I never had a chance,' Ben answered. 'Ellie – the Abo girl I mentioned – followed me down. She was right behind us all the time. If I'd said anything, she would've spilled it all to Molly.' He laughed. 'What she didn't know was that I had Trev tucked away inside Taronga.' He glanced at the thin-faced figure standing silently beside the door. 'I don't mind admitting I had something real special lined up for him before they started pushing me around.' He laughed again. 'But that's past history. He helped me over the fence and I locked him in a cage. I reckon we're quits now.'

Trev stirred restlessly, but he wasn't Ben's prime concern. Most of Ben's attention was on the squat shape at the far end of the garage. To his relief Chas abandoned the shadows, advancing with a slightly rolling gait.

'You've got yourself an agreement,' he said, no longer

161

trying to hide his enthusiasm. 'You help us get inside Taronga, and in exchange we wipe out the mob already in there. Afterwards you can look after the cats for us.' He paused, both fists bunching menacingly. 'All except one of them anyway. That bugger of a tiger! He's mine!'

Ben, thinking of the striped face staring at him in the torchlight, had to resist the impulse to defend Raja. 'You can sort that out afterwards,' he replied evasively. 'Let's get the raid over with first. When do we start?'

Chas's hands relaxed as he overcame his anger. 'I'll need time to bring some more men in.'

'How long?'

He stood pensively, his heavily muscled arms hanging slackly by his sides. 'A week,' he said at last. 'Exactly a week from tonight. We'll make the break-in an hour after sunset.'

'That's fine by me.'

'And you'll have everything ready? The power turned off? The cats locked up?'

Ben's hands suddenly felt hot and sticky. He knew this was the critical moment, on which everything hinged. 'And the wire too,' he added, 'right behind the restaurant – I'll start cutting a hole there for you. I won't finish it in case someone notices the gap. There'll just be a few strands for you to cut on the night.' He hesitated, steadying himself before going on: 'By the way, I'll need bolt-cutters to get through that heavy mesh. They're the kind of thing Molly keeps locked away. Could you let me have a pair?'

He was sure that Chas must have noticed the nervous tremble in his voice, but the hooded head merely turned towards Trev.

'Can you fix him up?'

'Sure, Chas. We'll collect a pair from the stores on the way back.'

'That's about it, then,' Chas said. 'I'll see you in a week's time.'

He held out his hand and Ben took it. Behind him, Trev was already opening the door.

'Don't you let me down now,' Chas said warningly, as a parting shot.

Ben was about to voice some easy assurance, but he had had enough of lies and betrayal for one evening and he chose instead to fall back on the simple truth. 'I'd be letting myself down as well, wouldn't I?' he answered, stepping quickly through the doorway.

The night air was noticeably cool and fresh. By contrast, his own body, covered with a slick of nervous sweat, felt strangely unclean, corrupted. Yet for once, the first time in years, he was untroubled by either guilt or regret. This, after all, was what he had wanted – a free, clear-eyed choice; the dark route he had elected to pursue.

When he reached the road he found that only Trev was waiting for him, the other three men having disappeared. That in itself was a sign of Chas's trust, and with growing confidence he followed Trev back along the maze of streets. Just before they reached the parkland bordering the harbour, his tall companion left the road and vanished into one of the half-ruined houses. He reappeared a few minutes later and placed a heavy pair of bolt-cutters in Ben's hands.

'Can you find your way from here?' he said gruffly.

Ben nodded, expecting him to hurry back to Chas. But he lingered there, shuffling his feet, acting undecided.

'What's the matter?' Ben asked.

'What you said back there,' he answered hesitantly, 'about having something special lined up for me when you locked me in the cage – that wasn't true, was it?'

But on this of all nights Ben was not seeking friendship, not from someone like Trev. 'Why not?' he said easily. 'I did owe you one, didn't I?'

Despite the darkness, he saw a suggestion of disappointment flit across the rodent-like features.

163

'Yeah, well I just thought I'd ask.'

Once he had gone, Ben, the bolt-cutters gripped tightly in both hands, walked across the park to the beach. He paused there for some time, staring out over the water. There was nothing wistful about his steady gaze; his mind nursing no secret longings for his old home. He was thinking only of the vastness of the ocean from which these harbour waters flowed, and of the huge mass of land behind him. The two great realities, earth and water, held in perfect balance at this point beneath his feet. Water views! The words alone suggestive of space and freedom.

Freedom! Was it as simple as that, he wondered, a straightforward desire to lay waste all the fences and restrictions that dated back to before Last Days? No, as far as he was concerned there was more at stake than that one word. He had no illusions about his own motives and role. Like it or not, he was the betrayer, the Judas. What he had always been. But with a difference this time. That difference locked in the weight of the bolt-cutters now cradled in the crook of his arm.

Bending down, he picked up a stone and flung it far out into the bay, the splash creating a widening circle of ripples that soon mingled and blended with the general turbulence of the water.

'Taronga!' he murmured aloud – aware, as he spoke, of the great mass of land pressing at his back; imagining Raja, his striped coat like pale fire in the starlight, pacing restlessly through its regenerating forests; his paws scuffing the dusty surface of its deserts.

CHAPTER FIFTEEN

Those seven days of waiting were totally unlike the rest of the time he had spent in Taronga. The real change, as he knew well enough, lay in himself, though still he couldn't avoid the suspicion that it was Taronga itself that had changed. Ever since Molly's mention of the Doomsday plan, it was as if the whole hillside had thrown off its former disguise of refuge and revealed its true underlying nature. This new, less benevolent image was something Ben found it difficult to live with. No longer could he enjoy walking along the deeply shaded lower paths, not with the lingering reek of death in the air. Nor was the rest of the park any more acceptable. On the upper paths he was confronted by the stark outline of the ruined city; while in the main body of the Zoo the many cages, which he had hardly been conscious of before, now challenged him at every turn – as did the armed men and women who herded the animals, their jungle-green uniforms always in evidence. Wherever he went, every sight and sound filled him with the unhappy conviction that he and all that he held dear were living on borrowed time.

He was no stranger to such a feeling. He had experienced it once before, when he had lived with his parents at Coogee, during Last Days. Then too the nights had been disturbed by screams, the days marked by a growing tension; he and his parents aware that the flimsy remains of peace and order could collapse at any moment.

Now, locked in Taronga with people like Molly and Steve, the ruthless survivors of Last Days, he felt as though he were living through that same process all over again. His only immediate escape was into sleep – his hours of rest, since the visit to Chas, not quite so plagued by nightmare as they had been. He still dreamed of the ambush on the road, of the wounded dingo, of the dog's trusting eyes, but those memories, although still painful, had lost some of their nightmare quality and he no longer awoke sweating and in anguish. Rather it was the waking world that he dreaded: a world of guns and cages and the certain promise of cruelty and violence.

Like Ellie, who had warned him weeks earlier about Taronga, he was now faced with the daily task of hiding his feelings from the people around him. It was always a relief to creep away with Ellie and discuss their plans for the night of the break-in. During those few brief hours he was free to speak his mind. For the rest of the time he had to carry on the charade of contentment.

There was no pretending with Raja, however. Increasingly sensitive to Ben's thoughts and moods, the tiger understood instinctively that some drastic change had taken place in him. Night by night he became less difficult to handle, the remains of his gnawing hatred gradually dissolving as he came to realize that Ben, in some inexplicable way, was a creature like himself – trapped, at bay before the other human beings. Yet that growing realization, although it removed much of the enmity between them, failed to establish any lasting trust. Still Raja held back, unsure, suspicious of this boy who had once imposed his will so ruthlessly upon him; the new and the old images of Ben existing side by side in his mind in a kind of uneasy alliance that bewildered him.

This strange mixture of familiarity and distrust was clearly

166

reflected in their regular confrontations. Each evening when Ben Called to him, he would respond eagerly at first, bounding across his cage towards the open door. Only when he caught sight of Ben's face would he hesitate, drawing up with a baffled growl, shaking his head from side to side. The cause of his disquiet was only too visible. The wound Ben had received had formed a dark brown scab that gave him an odd appearance: one half of his face unblemished, as it had always been; the other half deeply altered. It was that contrast which troubled Raja, echoing as it did his own internal conflict.

'Come, Raja, come,' Ben would murmur coaxingly.

And the tiger would creep forward, almost convinced by Ben's soothing tone, his burning eyes fixed upon the wound which ran from Ben's temple down to the line of his jaw. Then some slight movement would highlight the other half of Ben's face and he would pause, snarling in bewilderment, lashing out at this physical likeness of his old enemy and keeper.

There was nothing Ben could do to resolve the dilemma. Regardless of how he acted, Raja remained torn between acceptance and rejection of him.

'What can I do?' he asked Ellie in desperation.

'Give him time,' she said.

'We don't have much time,' he objected. 'It's running out.'

'Then why worry? What does it matter as long as we're successful in the end?'

But it did matter to Ben, though he would have found it difficult to explain why. More than anything else he wanted to win Raja's trust, as if that alone could put to rest the ghosts of the past, make a lasting peace with his guilty memories. And with each passing day – the remaining time slipping like fine sand through his fingers – his need to establish a trusting relationship with Raja grew ever more urgent.

Raja, meanwhile, was driven by a similar sense of urgency. Perplexed and also fascinated by his conflicting views of Ben, he again took to lying in wait for him: not now with thoughts of ambush, but merely to watch him, as though the repeated sight of Ben's face could solve the mystery of his identity. When Ben released him in the early dusk, he no longer made for the wall at the bottom of the slope. Instead, he followed Ben up to the restaurant: stealing through the bush that bordered the path; sometimes circling around towards the rotunda and peering out from its dark interior.

He would still be there, patiently waiting, in the early hours of each morning when, with everyone else asleep, Ben would open the upstairs window and crawl down the tiled roof, dropping silently onto the driveway. Without revealing his nearness, Raja would stalk around the end of the building, keeping the boy always in view; watching as the puny human arm groped for something on the wall and pulled it downwards – growling softly as blue sparks crackled in the darkness.

The first time that occurred, the night after his interview with Chas, Ben was not aware of Raja's presence until after he had cut the power controlling the alarm system. As he eased the switch to the 'off' position, he heard a rumbling growl and spun around. He fully expected Raja to charge and was ready to repulse the attack. But nothing happened, the animal content simply to watch him from a distance.

Ben continued to feel Raja's eyes upon him as he stole down the hillside. Several times, hearing a faint rustle of movement, he stopped and peered into the bushes; but it was impossible to separate the long striped body from the surrounding shadows and he soon hurried on. Ellie was already waiting for him when he reached their rendezvous point – a cage that had once housed wedge-tailed eagles, but which now, with the eagles long since flown, was used as a stall for small antelope.

'What kept you?' she asked impatiently.

168

He pointed back up the hillside. 'It's Raja, he's following me.'

'Is he dangerous?'

Ben probed questioningly into the darkness. 'No, not dangerous,' he said, trying to think of the right word to describe what he had just encountered. 'He's sort of . . . curious.'

'Then let's not worry about him,' she said decisively. 'Come on, we don't have much time. We can't leave the power off too long, just in case someone checks up.'

Together, they made for that part of the fence where they had previously dug the escape trench. Overgrown and sheltered from the rest of the park, it was as good a place as any for them to start. Dragging the bolt-cutters from the clump of bushes where they lay hidden, Ben set about cutting a large opening in the woven mesh of the fence. It was hard work, each metal strand having to be clipped through, and Ben soon passed the cutters to Ellie, the two of them taking it in turns, hurrying to complete as much of the job as possible, but at the same time taking great care not to damage any of the fine alarm wires.

Ben stepped back at last, his face and body streaming with sweat. 'That'll have to do for tonight.'

Between them they had almost finished cutting out a great opening in the fence. Only a few strands now held the cut-out portion in position; yet because of the ivy swarming all over the mesh, it was impossible to spot the damage.

'D'you think anyone'll notice?' Ellie asked.

'Not unless they lean against it, and that's not likely.'

Ben took the bolt-cutters and tossed them back into the bushes. Only then, as the heavy body crashed hastily away, did he remember about Raja.

'He must have been right there,' he said wonderingly, 'watching us all the time. So close!'

169

Ellie shrugged, not really concerned. 'At least he had a look at what we're doing,' she answered. 'Maybe that's a good thing. When the time comes, he'll be less likely to give us any trouble.'

'Let's hope so.'

But they had both misunderstood the reason for Raja's nearness. It wasn't their activity at the fence, but Ben himself who drew him – his brooding, amber-coloured eyes, as he had lain only paces away in the cover of the bushes, focussed exclusively on that human face in which he could discern both enemy and friend.

From then on he followed them every night, whether they were cutting the fence at the top of the hillside or on the far boundary overlooking the harbour. As they worked, he would edge forward, sometimes startling them by his nearness. He never attacked: his body poised, balanced, but with its great strength contained; his haunches gathered beneath him, ready for that final spring which he was too undecided to make.

It was the same on the sixth and final night of their secret activity. Ben and Ellie were working on the fence just behind the restaurant where Ben, true to his promise, had made a start on a hole just big enough for a man to crawl through.

'Why not leave it to Chas to cut?' Ellie suggested, anxious about being discovered now success was so near.

'I can't,' Ben said. 'This hole was my excuse for asking for the bolt-cutters. We don't want him getting suspicious.'

'Well don't cut too much,' Ellie advised. 'That way you'll slow them down a bit.'

He nodded, completing about two-thirds of the circle. 'That should look pretty convincing,' he said, ruffling the ivy back into place. 'It's up to Chas now.'

Shouldering the heavy bolt-cutters, he turned – only to find his way barred by Raja.

'Back, Raja,' Ellie murmured, fearing he was about to strike.

170

Neither Raja nor Ben heard her, each too obsessed with the other's nearness; and also too surprised to throw up any protective barrier. Defenceless, without reserve, they gazed into each other's eyes; not fully understanding what they saw; knowing only that they had reached a moment of choice. Yet it was too early, neither of them ready for it; and as though by mutual consent, they both backed warily away.

'Soon,' Ben whispered, not taking his eyes from the tiger, 'soon.'

The repetition of that one word seemed to sound a jangling note for both of them. Even as he spoke it, Ben felt uneasy; and Raja, moving almost too quickly for the eye to follow, leaped off into the darkness.

'What happened there?' Ellie asked, startled.

Again Ben barely heard her. With a sense of shame, he was remembering another occasion when he had repeated that one short word – 'soon'. He had been speaking to the dog, the night before they had ridden into Sydney; and then too he had meant it as an assurance, a kind of promise.

He looked directly at Ellie, her face, as always, open and without guile. 'I made a vow once,' he said slowly, 'that I'd never Call again. And soon afterwards I broke it.' He paused briefly. 'Well this time it's going to be different,' he went on in a determined voice. 'Whether or not things work out tomorrow night, it'll be the last time I'll ever Call. No matter what happens afterwards. I swear it.'

The shutters were in place, the lamps lit. Ben heard the back door open and close as Steve came in, the heavy bolts already being driven home.

'I've checked the alarm,' Steve called out.

Molly immediately began ringing through to the other centres, ensuring that all the animals were caged. Not until she had finished did she glance across at Ben. 'Get moving,' she said curtly, 'quick as you can.'

It was a sequence of events they had kept rigidly to ever

171

since the previous break-in. As usual Ben left the restaurant at a run, but this time he didn't hurry straight down to the tiger cages. When he had gone only a short distance he stopped and, in the failing light of early evening, doubled back to the restaurant where he crept silently along the back wall and turned off the power. That done, he made his way quickly to what had once been known as the rainfall aviary, a tall, airy, modern structure close to the upper ponds. Unlatching the end door, he pulled it open and breathed in the warm dusty smell of herbivorous animals. He could see little of the interior, but he could hear a steady munching and the rustle of hooved feet on the straw-strewn ground.

'Come,' he Called softly, 'come.'

There was another sound now, of animals lurching to their feet. He detected an initial, faint response of fear, and stilled it at once with another soothing Call. Already he could see the animals appearing out of the gloom: the elegant heads of antelope; the heavy, curving horns of the barbary sheep; the flaring, tree-like antlers of stags; the more familiar shapes of sheep and cattle. They came towards him in small tight-knit groups, quiet, trusting, following him out through the open door and along the winding paths.

In the gathering darkness he paused at other aviaries and cages where he released more animals: giraffes, camels, lamas, kangaroos, some of the larger antelope. Until soon there was a lengthy procession streaming along behind him, all of them docile and accepting of his leadership, silent but for the faint click of hooves on the hard surface.

Calling softly and persistently, he led them up the topmost path towards the former education centre, branching off to the left and following the line of the fence to where he knew Ellie was waiting.

She stepped out of the shadows ahead of him. 'I was getting worried,' she said in a low voice.

172

'It's all right,' he assured her. 'We still have time, and these are all the animals in the upper section. How've you been doing?'

She pointed back across the hillside. 'I've finished cutting the fence on the far boundary.'

'And here?'

But he could already see: just enough light remaining to show him the great hole in the fence, even the fine alarm wires cut through.

'Ah yes,' he said, but not moving, feeling suddenly less certain now that he was faced with an actual breach in Taronga's defences.

'We'd better get them through,' she suggested.

Still he didn't move – looking back along the line of animals that were waiting patiently for his decision; conscious, even in the deepening dusk, of their eyes upon him; their minds open, receptive, ready to obey.

'What's the matter?' Ellie asked.

She stepped towards him, her thin fingers grasping his arm, shaking him slightly, as though trying to awaken him from a trance.

'Some of them'll die out there,' he murmured, his voice heavy with misgiving. 'Perhaps most of them.'

'We've already been through all that,' she said quickly.

'I know. But they trust us. They . . . '

'Listen,' she interrupted, 'they're going to die in here too. You know that. At least they'll be free out there, they'll have a chance. Some of them'll make it to the bush.'

'And if they don't?'

She shook him again, more roughly. 'What are you trying to do?' she said angrily. 'Play at being God? The rest's not for us to decide. All we can do is what's best for them now.'

Their raised voices had begun to disturb the waiting animals, some of them throwing up their heads, others edging away from the fence. It was these signs of alarm, as much as Ellie's arguments, which restored some of Ben's resolve.

'I hope we're right,' he said, and walked rapidly through the opening and out into the light scrub beyond.

From there he Called to the animals while Ellie urged them on from behind. The leaders, a group of eland, stepped up to the hole and stopped, their nostrils flaring the wind, testing the strange scents which drifted in from the ruined city. They hesitated, sensing the broad, unexplored spaces that awaited them, the other animals pressing forward, pushing against them. Then, slowly and deliberately, they took their first steps out into the open, their flanks quivering with expectation.

'Go,' Ben commanded, 'go!'

With short surging leaps they swept past him, out into the danger and freedom of the night: their sudden rush causing a minor stampede, the rest of the animals bursting through the fence and crashing off in pursuit. Only the giraffes balked slightly, having to duck their long necks beneath the top of the opening; but once clear of the wire they too galloped away.

Ben walked slowly back into Taronga. He appeared dazed, frightened by what they had just achieved. By contrast Ellie was elated, too excited at first even to sympathize with him.

'We've done it!' she said happily. 'They're free! Whatever else happens tonight, it'll all be worthwhile.'

When he failed to respond, she took him by the shoulders and looked into his troubled eyes. 'Come on, Ben,' she encouraged him, 'there's a lot still to do.'

But momentarily all he could think of was the dog, abandoned and without protection within the savage heart of the city. 'What if . . . ?' he began uncertainly.

'It's too late for ifs,' she broke in. 'We've got to finish what we've started. If we stop now, people like Chas and Steve'll be

174

out there tomorrow hunting the animals down. Is that what you want?'

He shook his head. 'You know what I want,' he said more steadily.

'Then what are we standing here for? You said yourself, just freeing the animals isn't enough. We've got to make sure the cats are the only ones who follow them, and there's only one way of doing that. Bloody hell, Ben, it was your idea! A way of giving Raja and the rest of them the chance they deserve!'

That roused him completely: made him think not of the dog, but of Raja pacing restlessly within his cage. He looked about him, noting with concern how close to night it was.

'Here,' Ellie said, groping in the long grass, thrusting the bolt-cutters towards him. 'You'll need these. I'll see you in about half an hour, after I've got the animals out on the far side.'

'And the people in the house?'

'Don't worry,' she said with an uncertain smile, 'I haven't forgotten. I'll bring them over as soon as the shooting starts.'

He wanted to tell her to be careful, not to get involved in the fighting, but she had already gone, her lithe body flitting off into the shadows. He too began to run, back towards the restaurant – pausing outside only long enough to hide the bolt-cutters in a clump of bushes and then bursting in through the front door.

'What the hell!' Molly shouted as he rushed across the main room.

He stumbled against the counter, feigning breathless excitement. 'Something's going on,' he gasped, 'just outside the fence! People all over the place!'

'Which part of the fence?' Molly asked sharply.

He pointed in the direction of the kitchen. 'Right there, behind the building. I think they're going to break in.'

Molly looked at Steve who hurried to the stairs and

175

shouted. There was a clatter of footsteps and people came leaping down.

'Could you lead an armed group out there?' Molly asked Ben.

'Better not to,' he advised, 'not yet, anyway. I've got a bunch of the cats near that part of the fence. Ellie's out there with them, making sure they don't slink off. They should be able to handle it. But be ready just in case anyone gets through.'

While he was speaking, Steve began dragging boxes in from the next room and distributing guns and ammunition. For the first time ever he offered Ben a gun, but he refused it, already sidling towards the door.

'Where're you going now?' Molly called after him.

'I want to keep an eye on things.'

She frowned. 'Maybe you should stay in here for a while,' she advised. 'One of you out there should be enough.'

He felt a flutter of panic in the pit of his stomach. 'It's up to you,' he said carefully, knowing from experience that there was no point in openly opposing her. 'But with two of us, we'll stand a better chance of warning you if things get real bad.'

'I think he's right,' Steve cut in. 'If we know when they're coming, we can have a little reception party waiting.'

He raised one of the guns and cocked it, as if to demonstrate his point. Molly relaxed, a thin smile creasing her lips.

'All right,' she conceded, 'but keep your eyes peeled.'

'We won't miss a thing,' he promised her. 'If the situation does get rough, we can always bring people over from the house or down from up top.'

'That's good thinking,' Molly said. 'I'll tell them to be ready, just in case.'

As she reached for the phone, Ben scurried for the door, throwing the bolts and slamming it closed behind him.

It was almost dark now, later than he had bargained for, the minutes slipping away from him. There was no time to finish cutting the fence first, as he had intended. Retrieving the bolt-cutters from the bushes, he ran down to the elephant house where he flung the doors wide open. It was not easy hiding his sense of urgency, trying to appear calm and at ease, but he managed it somehow, Calling soothingly into the darkness. Once again the animals responded readily, moving out into the open, following him down towards the aviaries just below the tiger cages.

But already his task was becoming more difficult. The cats in the nearby cages, frustrated by their confinement and scenting the live game outside, began roaring angrily. And the animals following Ben, unnerved by the noise, milled about him in terror. Controlling them as best he could, he worked faster than ever, tugging open the mesh doors of the aviaries, adding more and more animals to the unruly procession. Soon he had freed all but the rhinos in the near corner of the park, and it was impossible to go down there now – not with the herd he had collected already on the point of rushing blindly away into the darkness.

Calling strongly and insistently, he set off at a run, animals of all shapes and sizes surging after him, jostling to keep up. Almost lost amongst the mass of heavy bodies and horned heads, he skirted the tiger cages and made for the weak point in the fence. Again the animals milled about him as he groped amongst the ivy, hastily locating the few uncut links in the mesh. It took him only a few minutes to snip through these – and even less to cut the fine alarm wires which stood out clear of the ivy. With the last strand severed, he pushed on the fence, expecting the whole section of cut mesh to fall easily away. But although it bulged outwards under the pressure, it remained in place, held there by the tangle of ivy.

'Come on!' he muttered desperately, heaving at the wire.

He knew he had little time left, and still there were Raja

177

and the other cats in the building to be released. Yet no matter how hard he pushed and heaved, still the coiling mass of greenery resisted him.

Panting, temporarily drained of energy, he leaned his forehead against the cool green leaves. And at that moment the sound he had been both dreading and anticipating burst out across the hillside: a sharp volley of gunfire, coming from somewhere near the restaurant.

CHAPTER SIXTEEN

The gunfire didn't make Ben panic, though it did challenge his plan of clearing Taronga and leaving the rival gangs to fight it out on the deserted hillside. Now, with his present escape route blocked, he was faced with the task of leading the herd across the park to one of the other cut sections of fence. He was not sure he could do that successfully, not with the constant noise of shooting in the background. And if the animals scattered, there was no knowing how long it would take to Call them together. Also, there was the delay involved, with Raja and the other predators still trapped in the cages. What would happen to them if Molly or Chas gained the upper hand and began to investigate? On finding the park almost empty, they might out of sheer malice decide to . . .

He cut short such thoughts, preferring not to consider them unless he had to; already planning the best route across the hillside. But he had reckoned without the will of the animals themselves.

The first shot had thrown them into a state of alarm, subsequent reports only increasing their terror. In the few seconds Ben needed to plan his next move, they had already passed beyond his control. Without the confining structure of a cage to protect them, threatened as much by the surrounding space as by the noise, they began crowding against each

179

other, deaf to Ben's entreaties. In vain he Called to them, pushing at the bodies pressing in upon him, his hands and then his fists beating at the tough furry hides. But his efforts had the reverse of the effect he intended. One huge, shaggy-coated bison, startled by the unexpected touch of his hand, whirled and lunged, the blunt forehead sending him crashing into the ivy-covered mesh. A young steer lurched into the space he had just occupied; its place in turn being taken by other animals; that initial movement creating a wave-like effect, the whole herd crowding in towards the fence.

Ben, pinned against the ivy-covered mesh, could hardly breathe, the weight of heavy bodies placing almost unbearable pressure on his stomach and chest. Helpless, unable even to cry out in protest, he had a fleeting vision of being crushed to death. But all at once there was a tearing noise as the thick strands of ivy gave way before the combined onslaught, and Ben was pitched backwards into open space, the herd surging through the gap after him. Shadowy legs and bodies filled his vision, blotting out the starlit sky. Then, eyes tightly closed, he rolled over and curled himself into a ball, his head buried in his arms as the herd swept over him.

They seemed to take an unbearable time to pass, the drum of their hoofbeats becoming confused in his mind with the distant gunshots, so that he remained curled up and still long after they had gone. When at last he sat up there was no sign of them, the whole herd having bolted into the cover of the National Park bordering that side of Taronga.

Cut and bruised, his body aching from the pummelling it had just taken, he rose shakily to his feet. He barely knew where he was – the fence, the outline of the bushes, the glimmer of stars, all strangely blurred. In the background he could hear shooting, he even understood vaguely what it signified, but it failed to convey any sense of urgency to him. There was another sound too, low and booming, which he had difficulty in placing. Only as his head slowly cleared did he recognize it: the roar of the cats, amplified by the tunnel.

Staggering slightly, he ran to the building housing their cages. The cats, incensed by the nearby conflict, were in a frenzy of activity, leaping frantically around their cages, some of them crashing wildly into the bars. Even in his dazed condition he realized that if he let them leave the building ahead of him, he would lose them. Pulling the double doors closed, he ran the length of the tunnel and slid Raja's door up first – holding the animals at bay as he worked his way back towards the entrance. With the tunnel closed off, they made no attempt to rush him. Only towards the end was he in real danger, a line of snarling cats edging forward as he struggled to reopen the heavy doors. Had Raja chosen to challenge him at that instant, he would have had little chance; but the tiger, still as fascinated and confused by Ben as he had been all week, held back; and his restraint had a dampening effect on the others.

Much the same happened when Ben drew them outside. Aroused by the sputter of gunfire, they struggled to break free, eager to join the conflict where, as experience had taught them, there would be food in plenty. But again Raja showed little readiness to oppose Ben. With Ranee beside him and the others following close behind, he allowed himself to be led across the hillside. Their progress was slow until they scented the herd; then it was all Ben could do to hold them back. One after another, they overtook him, bounding through the screen of bushes and out into the darkness beyond the fence.

Only Raja stopped at the opening. Like the others, he was attracted by the scent of game; and more than that, by the salt-laden breeze which conveyed to him a tangible sense of that freedom he yearned for. He had only to step beyond the wire and his long confinement would be over – the land, the long curving line of the shore, his to roam at will. Yet still he lingered there at the edge of Taronga, as if loath to leave it;

181

his mind, previously so single in its purpose, now divided against itself; his eyes, dark with bewilderment, turned towards the enigmatic figure of Ben.

Ben was tempted to Call him back, to draw him just once more, in the hope that the last barrier separating them would come crashing down and he would perceive in those amber eyes what he had taken so much for granted in the eyes of the dog. It was a vain hope, as he soon acknowledged – such dreams belonging to the past, not to the strident urgency of the present. And instead of luring the tiger, he Called softly, 'Go . . . go,' impelling him out into the vastness of the night.

That selfless action only increased Raja's bewilderment, clashing as it did with his former image of Ben as the hated jailer. Letting out a roar of pain and anger, he swatted ferociously at the empty air, venting his resentment not of Ben, but of a situation he could no longer comprehend, his simple, vigorous intelligence thwarted beyond endurance.

'For God's sake get out of here!' Ben yelled, equally pained at seeing him so troubled.

He scrabbled blindly in the shadows, picking up sticks and tufts of grass and hurling them at the broad, striped face which had haunted him throughout his months in Taronga. And slowly Raja backed away, edging reluctantly out through the opening. There, once again, he paused and looked towards Ben, sidling off into the bush only when Ranee growled to him from the darkness.

With Raja gone, Taronga felt peculiarly empty, a meaning-less stretch of hillside, the continued noise of gunfire making it seem more desolate. Ben would have liked to walk out through the opening just as Raja had done, and leave it for ever; but there was still Ellie to be considered, as well as the final, most distasteful part of his plan.

It was the closing episode which he dreaded most of all and had been trying hard until now not to think about. Reluctantly, he faced up to the necessity of the moment. Whether

182

he liked it or not, the time had come for him to betray the people in the entrance building, much as Ellie would already be betraying those left in the house – his task, and hers, to lure the rest of Molly's supporters to the desperate and probably fatal struggle taking place around the restaurant. He flinched away from the idea, yet knew that if the animals were to make good their escape, without fear of recapture, then it had to be carried through; everything Taronga now stood for smashed completely. The final betrayal – that was how he thought of it, this last part of his plan: a betrayal designed to wipe out all previous treacheries in a last convulsive recreation of Last Days.

His attention was attracted by a faint glow just above the line of the trees. Firelight! The restaurant already burning! Once again he had very little time in which to act. Putting his doubts forcibly aside, he began running uphill, choosing a path that would take him around the fighting and up towards the entrance building. But the further he went, the more he was racked by misgivings. He could see the blaze of the restaurant clearly now, over to his right: one whole wing burning fiercely; armed figures silhouetted against the leaping flames; some of them still firing; others, obviously wounded, staggering away.

Ben slithered to a stop, his mind grappling with his own earlier resolve. How could he lead people towards that inferno? Cut short their lives in cold blood? It was too deliberate, too calculating. Far from wiping out past acts of betrayal, it would merely add to them.

'No!' he groaned aloud, knowing that he could not go through with it, whatever the risk to the animals. To set the safety of so many animals against the lives of so many human beings was an impossibility. An absurd equation that could never be solved, by him or anyone.

Almost guiltily, he turned back – and was startled by someone flitting silently across his path. It was Ellie, combing

183

the hillside in search of him.

'Ben?' she called hesitantly.

She came slowly towards him, clearly shocked by his appearance: his shirt ripped to shreds, his arms and body cut and bruised from where the herd had stampeded over him.

'Are you all right?' she asked.

'I can't go through with it, Ellie,' he broke out, ignoring her show of concern. 'I know we agreed – that we'd finish them off, the way they'd finish us given the chance. But I'm not leading them into that! I don't care what . . . '

She placed her fingers gently on his mouth, silencing him. 'You don't have to,' she said, her voice alone telling him plainly that she had reached the same conclusion. 'When I saw what it was like here, I tried to turn them back – the ones from the house – but they wouldn't listen. And a few minutes ago I saw the rest, from up in the entrance building, creeping down towards the fire.'

'Shouldn't we try and warn them?' he asked half-heartedly.

'It's too late. And anyway it wouldn't do any good. This is what they want. Last Days. They'd have come to this whether we'd been here or not.'

The flames were leaping towards the sky now, figures rushing out through burning doorways, the explosive crackle of gunfire rising to a crescendo.

With his weirdly divided face brilliantly lit by the fire, Ben turned desperately towards her. 'Couldn't we have stopped it?' he asked in agonized tones. 'Couldn't we . . . ?'

'No,' she cut in. And then more loudly, her voice shrill with defiance, 'No! They didn't leave us any other choice! They never have done! Never, since the first ships sailed into that harbour down there. Just this once, though, we've answered them. We've rescued something from the mess they left us. Well haven't we?'

He looked towards the fire – the red and yellow flames etched against the black sky reminding him of Raja: the long powerful body, beautifully striped, poised in the jagged opening in the fence, with not just the chaotic remains of Sydney, but the whole of Australia beyond.

'Yes, we've rescued something,' he assented. And as a sudden afterthought: 'But we haven't finished yet. There are still the rhinos.'

Ellie turned resolutely away from the battle which had now reached a fever pitch, curses and yells accompanying the regular stutter of shots, the whole scene like a vision of hell, with the warring figures prancing grotesquely before the roaring flames.

'Everything's gone from my side,' she answered. 'The rhinos are the last. I'll come and help.'

Together, as on the night Ben had entered Taronga, they ran rapidly along the winding paths, making for the near, lower corner where the rhinos were housed. The animals were outside in the concrete courtyard when they arrived – a big male, a female, and a young calf of four or five months – all of them trotting restlessly to and fro, disturbed by the distant noise. Unlatching the metal gate, Ellie swung it open, while Ben called coaxingly to the nervous animals. They emerged with a kind of cautious belligerence, their tails stiff and straight behind them, their heads held high, scenting the night air, small piggy eyes peering into the darkness.

'Come,' Ben signalled gently, and led the way back up the hill, Ellie jogging along beside him.

By then, the last desperate struggle around the restaurant had nearly reached its bloody conclusion. Only a few random shots broke the silence, and in the more peaceful atmosphere the rhinos were easy to handle. But although the fight was almost over, the restaurant was still blazing fiercely, and as they neared the hole in the fence the breeze carried the smell of burning down towards them. The effect on the rhinos was to make them veer away, letting out sharp coughing grunts of protest.

'Maybe we should take them to the other side of the park,' Ellie suggested.

'It's all right,' Ben said. 'I think I can hold them. And we're nearly there.'

Using all his skill, he lured them up the last stretch of hillside. A thick clump of bushes was all that separated them from the gaping hole in the fence. With the male in the lead, they pushed into the bushes and stopped, the glare from the fire plain enough even to their poor vision.

'Sneak round behind them,' Ben murmured. 'Try and drive them forward. Once they see the hole, they'll make a run for it.'

She crept away, leaving Ben out in the open, his back to the fence, the gaping hole to his right – the rhinos' path to freedom totally unobstructed.

'Come,' he repeated, and was relieved to see the bushes shake violently, the great pointed horn on the male rhino's snout appearing briefly above the dense foliage.

With just a little more effort he was sure he could make them emerge: his mind so intent on the task that he didn't hear the approaching footsteps. Not at first. Only when they stopped, replaced by laboured breathing, did he spin around. Molly was standing a few paces away, an automatic rifle gripped in both hands. Her hair and clothes had been singed by the flames, her face smudged with soot, a dark splotch of blood staining her side. She was looking not at Ben, but at the damaged fence, a bitter expression on her face. She staggered to the opening and turned towards him.

'You little bastard!' she said, spitting the words out. 'So this is what it was all about!'

The harsh lines on her face twisted into a snarling grimace as she slowly raised the gun. Before she could pull the trigger there was a frantic rustling in the bushes near by. Distracted, she whirled around, searching the darkness; and Ben, making the most of the opportunity, began sidling away, his foot

186

striking something hard and cold in the tangle of grass. He knew what it was without looking, his hands groping downwards as the bushes were again shaken, the long prehistoric head of the male rhino thrusting through the thick veil of leaves. Ben's fingers closed around the handles of the bolt-cutters at exactly the instant that Molly snapped the rifle up to her shoulder. Even from his position, crouched slightly to one side, he could tell that she was aiming directly at the broad, vulnerable space beneath the thrusting head; and swinging his whole body forward with the effort, he flung the heavy bolt-cutters straight at her. They failed to hit their mark, flying harmlessly past her shoulder, but they startled her enough to make the barrel of the rifle ride up, the burst of automatic fire tearing through the sparse foliage above the rhino's head.

It was the one and only chance she had. There was an explosive, coughing grunt and the rhino came crashing stiff-legged through the screen of bushes. Whether he was intent upon charging Molly was never clear. Possibly his near-sighted vision picked up Molly and the hole in the fence at the same time, the two objects blurring into one; because he made straight for the opening, never for a second slackening his pace; his huge head jerking down and then up, the vicious horn catching Molly in the side and tossing her effortlessly into the air, her arms and legs flailing like the boneless limbs of a child's soft toy.

She didn't simply fall. Crashing against the upper, barbed-wire section of the fence, she hung there for several seconds, her clothing tangled in the knotted barbs. Then, with painful slowness, she toppled forward and down, her body bouncing off the broad back of the female rhino who was hurrying in pursuit of her mate, the calf cowering against her side. When at last Molly hit the ground, she lay very still, one arm twisted beneath her, the other stretched out, two fingers still clinging to the trigger guard of the rifle, as though even in the act of

187

dying she could not relinquish her hold upon the destructive symbol by which she had lived.

Ben, too shocked to move, remained crouching in the grass as Ellie came running around the bushes.

'What's going ... ?' she began, and stopped as she saw Molly lying before her. Kneeling down, she reached out and delicately touched the scorched, grimy cheek – Molly's eyes flickering open and closed, her mouth forming words Ellie could not make out. 'She's alive,' she said to Ben. 'She's trying to tell us something.'

Ellie bent closer, and this time the words, a mere breath of sound, just reached her: 'Last Days ... '

Molly took a shuddering breath, as if intending to add something more. But like so many of her own victims, ambushed within the confines of Taronga, she was denied the opportunity either to plead or to explain. There was a further sound of footsteps, heavier, more halting, and Chas limped into the clearing. He had been wounded in the leg, and as with Molly his clothes and skin were singed and blackened. At some stage in the fight he must have lost his rifle or run out of ammunition, because he was armed only with a long-bladed knife.

'Where is she?' he shouted hoarsely. His voice, muffled by the balaclava, was demented with rage.

Ellie leaped back defensively, but he barely noticed her. He was concerned only with the figure lying stretched out in the grass, recognizing it as the body of the woman who had thwarted him for so long, finally snatching victory from him on the night of his hoped-for triumph. As he gazed angrily at her, her cold green eyes again flickered open, staring back at him through the gloom, briefly hardening into focus.

'You!' he burst out, tightening his grip on the knife. 'You! You're going to pay ... pay ... !'

He lunged forward, his wounded leg almost buckling beneath him, making him lurch unsteadily to one side, so that to an onlooker he could just as easily have been running at the two young people as at Molly. It was that tiny mischance which cost him his life. For with a grating roar, Raja, until then hiding in the bush bordering the fence, held to this hated place by his own baffling uncertainty, charged back through the opening and struck.

'No, Raja!' Ben yelled.

His familiar voice, ringing out so unexpectedly, was just sufficient to make the tiger hesitate. The heavy paw, faltering in mid-swing, fanned past its intended target, the raking claws snagging in the greasy wool of the balaclava and tearing it away.

Mesmerized with terror, caught up in a nightmare he had already lived through once before, Chas stood stock still, eyes wide and staring, waiting for the inevitable blow to fall. Except that there never was another blow, Raja rearing back at the sudden appearance of this horribly deformed face. It was the second such bewildering transformation he had witnessed within Taronga: his image of humanity wavering, undergoing a strange process of change that eluded his burning hatred; leaving him free at last, as free as Ben and Ellie could have desired.

Snarling and spitting, he edged backwards, his paws brushing past Molly's shoulder, briefly recalling her from the slow drift into unconsciousness. Her eyes flickered open yet again, in time to see the terrifying head passing above her. Her reaction was instantaneous, the instincts of a lifetime crowding through the fog of pain. With what little strength she still retained, her outflung arm heaved the rifle upwards, her fingers tightening on the trigger. There was a stutter of fire, the rifle, with nothing to brace it against the recoil, swinging through a shallow arc that narrowly excluded Raja's head, centring on the thick-set body of Chas.

With a whirl of movement, Raja was gone: leaping back through the gap in the fence even before Molly's now lifeless

189

fingers relaxed their convulsive grip on the rifle. In the ensuing stillness Chas's body sank down beside that of his enemy, he and Molly as close to each other in death as they had truly been in life. Only Ellie and Ben remained, clinging to one another in the silvery starlight, surrounded by the silent, empty spaces of Taronga – the last blush of the dying fire just showing in the sky above the trees.

CHAPTER SEVENTEEN

As the sky paled, pink tufts of cloud appearing on the eastern horizon, Ben and Ellie emerged from the wilderness of overgrown gardens and stopped before a gaunt brick and concrete structure. It had once been a six-storey block of units, but now, abandoned and looted, its windows and doors smashed, it was more like the tower of some ruined fortress, its blunt outline rising above the lush growth which had almost submerged most of the surrounding rooftops.

Ellie peered through the front doorway into the dimly lit entrance hall. 'It's a bit like a cave inside,' she said a little fearfully.

'Better than most of the houses, though,' Ben answered. 'At least the ceilings haven't fallen in.'

Easing past her, he led the way into one of the flats. Even with the day breaking outside, the rooms were dark, the smallish window openings choked by bushes and vines.

'This should do us,' he commented, slipping the heavy rucksack from his shoulders and depositing it in one corner.

Ellie also put down her load, and for the next few minutes they busied themselves clearing a space in what had once been the living room, sweeping fragments of glass and crockery and pieces of smashed furniture to one side. When they had finished, they dragged over a square of old carpet

191

and spread it out.

'Ugh!' Ellie complained. 'It smells.'

'It's either this or the hard floor.'

She shrugged. 'I'll settle for the carpet. I ache enough already without lying on a rock-hard floor all day.'

They sank down onto the carpet, neither of them bothering about food for a while, content merely to rest; sitting with their shoulders almost touching, their backs leaning against the inner wall.

It was four nights since they had left Taronga – nights in which they had travelled not along the open roads, but through the burgeoning wilderness which was rapidly reclaiming the once flourishing city. Forcing a path through the dense undergrowth of back gardens and parks had proved to be slow, hard work. Yet it was preferable to the dangers of the road and so far they had seen no sign of any other human beings. Just occasionally they had glimpsed familiar shapes flitting away through the shadows ahead of them, the animals of Taronga choosing the same slow but safe route out of the city.

They were both thinking about the animals now, as they sat side by side in the green-tinged gloom. Ellie glanced at Ben, as if sensing his thoughts.

'The animals,' she murmured, 'they're escaping, the way we hoped.'

He nodded, remembering a large heavy body gliding through the twilight, disappearing behind the trailing limbs of a tall rose gum. 'That last one we saw, what d'you think it was?' he asked. 'A bison? One of the antelope?'

'I'm not sure. But it was something pretty big.' She laughed happily at the idea, adding, 'Not the kind of animal you expect to see in Australia.'

He looked at her wonderingly. 'And doesn't that worry you?'

'Should it?'

He hesitated. 'Well originally this was your country,' he began awkwardly. 'I mean, your people have been here for thousands of years. You said yourself that their lives have been sort of tied in with everything that's been going on here. And now it's all about to change, after what we've done. The animals we've released are going to breed and start competing with the marsupials; and the cats'll kill anything not quick enough to get out of the way. Whole species will disappear. And that's only the beginning. Even the plants will alter because of the different feeding habits. From now on nothing's ever going to be the same again.'

'Yes, I've thought about that too,' Ellie said quietly. 'I've tried to work out what my dad would have said.'

'And?'

'I think he'd have accepted it.'

'Why?'

'Well, there've been other changes in Australia before this. The Aboriginals brought the dingo here thousands of years ago – think of the difference that must have made. Then there was the coming of the Whites, with their own plants and animals.'

'Yes, but those changes don't excuse what we've done,' Ben interrupted her. 'How do we know our decision was the right one?'

She paused before replying, gazing with obvious distaste at the wreckage all about her. 'It was the right decision for me,' she said at last. She indicated the general disorder of the room. 'After this, there had to be some sort of beginning. And you can't have beginnings without change.'

'A beginning,' he repeated pensively.

'Well isn't it?'

'For you maybe.'

'And for you?'

He ran a hand distractedly through his hair. 'It's hard to say. Perhaps more of an ending than anything else.'

193

'I don't get that. An end to what?'

'Something that started a long time ago, when I first met Greg, out there beyond the mountains.'

Hearing the troubled note in his voice, she said nothing more. Already the sun had risen, the sound of birdsong very loud in the stillness of the morning.

'Time for something to eat,' she said.

She went to their rucksacks and took out two of the cans they had brought with them from the emergency store at Taronga. Not wanting to risk a fire, they ate the food cold, spooning it straight from the cans, and then washed it down with the musty-tasting water in their canvas bags. Afterwards, tired from the previous night's journey, they curled up on the square of carpet and went quickly to sleep.

They awoke in the late afternoon, the dark-green quality of the light telling them that the sun was not far from setting. Ellie sat up and stretched, feeling suddenly trapped by the gloomy confinement of the room.

'I'll be glad to get out of this city,' she said, 'to where there's some real space. How far d'you reckon we are from the mountains?'

'There's one way of checking up,' Ben answered, yawning sleepily. 'We could go to the top of the building and have a look.'

'Good idea.'

Leaping up, she made straight for the doorway, Ben following more slowly. She was waiting for him in the entrace hall, at the foot of the stairs, and together they climbed steadily upwards, floor by floor, until they reached the top. There was no door leading onto the roof, but from one of the units they had a clear view to the Blue Mountains. The forest-clad slopes were far closer than they had expected, a vast green-black expanse, faintly tinged with gold by the setting sun whose lower edge was hovering just above the horizon.

'We'll easily get to the foothills by morning,' Ellie said.

'From then on we'll make far better time. We should have enough food to reach that secret underground store you told me about.'

'And after that?' he asked, because the long-term future was not something they had discussed.

'Keep going west, I think. Through the settled farmland, out into the dry mulga country.'

'Why so far?'

'It's hard country to survive in. There'll be hardly any other people. We should be safe there for a year or two, until everything settles down a bit.'

He wanted to ask her how they were going to survive in such a harsh environment; whether she knew enough about the survival techniques of her own people to see them through. But before he could frame a question, there was a stir of movement somewhere in the building behind them.

'What was that?' he asked.

A soft hiss of warning escaped from Ellie's lips, one hand beckoning for him to follow as she glided across the room. Just as she reached the door there was another faint sound, much closer this time. With a cry of astonishment, she leaped through the opening, making rapidly for the head of the stairs.

'Ben, quick!' she called out.

But Ben, still only half way towards the door, was arrested by a familiar, rank odour. He knew the cause of it even before the massive head and forepaws slid into view, blocking the doorway.

'Raja!' he breathed out, that one word expressing not only surprise and fear, but also an odd kind of relief.

The animal was looking straight at him, the amber eyes flashing gold as they caught and held the flaming image of the setting sun. The same golden light bathed the whole face, making the barred pattern of cheeks and snout shimmer and glow, as if on fire. There was a low snarl, as familiar to Ben as

195

the rank feline smell, and the long body, sinking into a half-crouch, began creeping towards him.

All Ben's deepest instincts urged him to halt the advance with a silent command. Only one small part of himself, a tiny background voice, resisted the temptation, reminding him of a vow he had made and must keep. It was that voice which prevailed, blocking all his frantic attempts to force the tiger into submission.

'Raja,' he said again, the murmured name neither a plea nor a protest: merely the final plain statement of a fact which could no longer be avoided.

Steeling himself for what must follow, he backed away as far as the window and waited; passive, unresisting; watching as the golden, sun-filled eyes closed in on him. Somewhere beyond those eyes, on the far side of the room, there was a dark flicker of disturbance, too vague and distant to distract him.

'Call to him, Ben!' Ellie shrieked. 'Make him stop!'

He understood what was being demanded of him; but equally he realized that was no longer the way. He had spoken to Ellie of endings, and here, at last, was where the miseries and failures of the past must end. With what courage and faith remained to him, he stood perfectly still, his trembling lips closed and silent, watching as the advancing face loomed ever nearer, growing larger and more terrible with each step. That deadly advance ceased at last, but with the face so close to him now that, try as he might, Ben could no longer hold it in focus; its familiar outlines twisting and distorting into the likeness of all the animals he had ever lured. One by one he seemed to glimpse them in those blurred, distorted features: kangaroo, dingo, dog.

Ben let out a sob of recognition and slumped to his knees, aware that this after all was the end of his journey; his flight from Greg leading only to this. All those dead creatures exacting payment from him here and now. He could not help but acknowledge the justice of it, and he lowered his head, his shoulders and arms going slack and still. A blast of hot breath fanned his cheeks, accompanied by a rumbling growl; and in that last split-second, which he truly believed was all the time left to him, he glanced up. The striped lips were curled up and back, revealing long yellow-white canines; one paw was raised, about to strike. Everything was as he imagined it must be – all, that is, except for the eyes. Pools of yellow light, liquid and soft, almost trusting; nothing like his image of them. More like the eyes . . . like the eyes of . . .

He was not given time even to complete that one brief thought. Fascinated, he watched the broad, splayed paw sweep round towards him, the dark pads, momentarily caught in the glare of sunlight, looking oddly pliant and soft. He braced himself, ready for the blow which would crush out his life. Yet when the paw struck, it wasn't with the force of anger or hatred: it was far gentler than that; the cushioned pads cuffing him on the side of the head, as if in warning, hitting him only hard enough to tip him off balance. He felt himself drifting sideways and down; his body rolling beneath the still raised paw; his upturned face staring at the downy underside of Raja's head and chest.

For a full minute neither of them moved: Ben lying passively beneath the great striped body; Raja gazing into the setting sun, his eyes and coat aflame in its glowing light. Again the tiger growled, the sound rumbling deep in his throat. Then, with painstaking care, he stepped over Ben; the long body passing above him; the heavy tail flicking gently across his face.

Slowly, as from a protracted dream, Ben sat up. He found himself staring at what remained of an old wardrobe, its full-length mirror starred with cracks, but with enough of the glass left for him to see his own face. The long unsightly scab running from temple to jawline was still there, beginning to dry out now; some of it already flaking away, allowing the

197

fresh pink skin to show through, unscarred, like some new part of himself emerging from the wounds and ravages of the past.

He climbed stiffly to his feet as Ellie ran across the room. Flinging her arms about his neck, she hugged him briefly, hardly able to believe he was still alive.

'Are you all right?' she burst out.

He smiled reassuringly. 'I'm fine. Really.'

'I thought he was going to kill you. But then when he did strike, it was more like . . . like a sort of love pat.'

'Yes,' he said thoughtfully, 'perhaps it was that as well.'

She looked at his face, sensing some difference in him. 'What else was it?' she asked.

Ben didn't answer her directly. 'You know what we were talking about this morning,' he said. 'Well you were right. Letting the animals go wasn't just an ending. It was a beginning, for me too.'

'The beginning of what?'

He smiled again, no longer troubled by what awaited them beyond the mountains. 'Who knows? It's not only the animals that'll have to adapt. We'll have to as well. Anything can happen now. Anything.'

There was no hint of foreboding in his voice: only a thrill of anticipation and promise. While far beneath them, their coats aflame in the golden light that still flooded out across the plains, Raja and Ranee stole silently towards the mountains, moving deeper and deeper into the land, as though marking out those new, as yet invisible paths along which Ben and Ellie were soon to wander.

NOTE TO THE READER

Taronga Zoo, as I'm sure most of my Australian readers are aware, is a very real place and not just a figment of my imagination. I have tampered with its geography as little as possible, and only then to make my story more feasible. Thus, I have suggested that all the Zoo buildings are contained by the outer fence, even though that is not strictly true. Also, I have described the Zoo as it was before its most recent alterations, largely because that was how I first came to know it. I hope I may be forgiven for such small departures from the literal truth. Here, as in previous books, my intention has been to capture the spirit of a particular setting, not simply to give a factual description of it. I think I need hardly add that the characters in my book are fictional, and any resemblance which may exist between them and the personnel at the Zoo is purely coincidental.

Lastly, some mention must be made of the poet and visionary, William Blake. Nowhere in the novel itself have I referred to him directly; but those who know his work will recognize that, in my descriptions of Raja and Ranee, I am as indebted to him as I am to the beautiful tigers that inhabit Taronga.

Victor Kelleher, 1986

ABOUT THE AUTHOR

Victor Kelleher was born in London and spent his early childhood there. As a teenager, he travelled to Africa where he lived for twenty years, spending a lot of time in the bush, and hitch-hiking all over southern Africa. He was in his mid-thirties and living in New Zealand when he began to write, prompted by homesickness for Africa. Since 1976 he has lived in Australia. His first book for young people was *Forbidden Paths of Thual*. Since then he has written many outstanding novels for children.

Of his writing, Victor Kelleher says: 'I suppose at the most personal level I enjoy recreating the kind of "fabulous world" which delighted me as a child. Like many writers before me, I have tapped into a potent, enduring body of legend, which I first encountered as a child and which has continued to hold sway over me.'

Victor now lives in Sydney and is a full-time writer. *Taronga* was named an Honour Book in the 1987 Australian Children's Book of the Year Awards. More recently, Victor's novel *Brother Night* was an Honour Book in the 1991 Australian Children's Book of the Year Awards for older readers, and *Del-Del* was also shortlisted for the 1992 awards. His latest novel for older readers is *To the Dark Tower*.

MORE GREAT READING FROM PUFFIN

☆ ☆

ALSO BY VICTOR KELLEHER

The Red King

The Red King uses disease and death to control his people. One small circus troupe sets out on the impossible task of destroying the all-powerful leader.

Shortlisted for the 1990 Australian Children's Book of the Year Award. Joint runner-up in the 1990 SA Festival Awards. Shortlisted for the 1990 Australian Science Fiction Achievement Award.

Baily's Bones

Alex and Dee unwittingly become involved in a re-enactment of the past when they discover the bones of old Frank Baily.

Shortlisted for the 1989 NSW Premier's Literary Award. Joint runner-up in the 1990 SA Festival Awards.

The Makers

No one has ever seen the Makers, unknown rulers of the Keep, until the day Jeth is unjustly accused of breaking the laws of combat.

Shortlisted for the 1988 Australian Children's Book of the Year Award. Winner of the 1989 Peace Prize for Literature. Shortlisted for the 1988 NSW Premier's Literary Award and the 1988 Australian Science Fiction Achievement Award.

The Green Piper

Two teenagers and an old man are lured by a strange melody and discover something bewildering and sinister.